## Stornoway, Isle of Lewis

STORNOWAY is the main town on the Isle of Lewis and is also the home of the Western Isles Council. Just over 6,000 people live in the town, which represents about a third of the island's total population. The economy is a mix of traditional businesses like fishing, Harris Tweed and farming, with more recent influences like tourism, the oil industry and commerce brought about by the digital revolution and communications.

Stornoway is the main port on the island, due to its sheltered location, with the ferry to Ullapool a regular visitor. The sheltered harbour is the reason for Stornoway's existence and was named "Steering Bay" by the visiting Vikings which, when phonetically translated, became the name Stornoway.

As the primary ferry port for the Outer Hebrides, over 95% of all visitors to the Isle of Lewis travel through Stornoway harbour and it is a regular port of call for visiting cruise ships. ■

## Dear Readers...

**WELCOME** to "The People's Friend" Annual 2015, which we've put together with you in mind to ensure you enjoy a feast of super reading. Many of your favourite authors are among these 25 brand-new stories, and we have 14 seasonal poems for you to settle back and enjoy.

Our delightful J. Campbell Kerr paintings will whisk you on a tour around Britain, and we also take a nostalgic look back at our favourite childhood annuals.

We're certain you're going to love this year's Annual, but don't forget to pick up your regular "Friend" for more great reading, with super features and a fantastic story for every day of the week!

*Angela*

Angela Gilchrist, Editor

# Contents

## Complete Stories

# Poetry

p146

p174

# J.Campbell Kerr Paintings

# Annual Events

# Beyond The Blue Horizon

## by Annie Harris.

I'M sure you'll love our new Fliss Wild Rose Serum." Caroline smiled at her middle-aged customer as she handed her the package. "It is a bit pricey, I know, but it's very effective."

When the customer had gone, she looked at her watch. Time to close the shop.

"That's it, girls." She pulled down the pretty pink and silver blinds. "See you tomorrow."

"'Bye!" Young Trish shot off – as usual she had plans – but the other assistant, Jan, lingered, fidgeting with the counter display.

"Um, Caro, have you seen the new Fliss house mag?"

"No, I haven't had time. Is there anything interesting in it?"

Fliss was one of the retail success stories of the decade. The pretty design of its shops made it stand out on all the high streets and malls where they had opened, and its pure, high-quality products had quickly gained a good reputation. The business had been started by two sisters, Felicity and Lisa – hence the name – both with long careers as top beauticians behind them.

CAROLINE had drifted into Fliss almost by accident. Coming from a broken home and brought up by a succession of foster-parents, she'd been insecure and difficult as a youngster – angry with life.

Although she had gone to college, encouraged by teachers determined that she should fulfil the potential they could see in her, she had dropped out and taken a series of dead-end jobs. However, something amazing had happened when, in time, she'd joined Fliss as an assistant. She and the place had just clicked, and she had blossomed, rapidly rising to store manager.

Now Craig was talking of her as an area manager, like himself.

Craig . . . She smiled to herself. But then she remembered Jan.

"Sorry, you were talking about the magazine. Why do you ask?" she repeated.

"Oh, they're hoping to branch out in Australia. Felicity was there for years, apparently – had a salon in Sydney. Anyway, they're looking for someone to go out there and establish the first shop. And I was thinking –" She hesitated. "Why don't you apply? You're so good!"

*Illustration by John Hancock.*

"Not that good, I'm sure." Caroline laughed. "In any case, I'm perfectly happy here."

"Caro?" Jan's good-natured face was creased with anxiety. "Do you mind if I tell you something? My mum said I shouldn't say anything, but I think you ought to know that Mr Johnson . . ."

"Craig?"

"Yes. Well, I know you're, er, close, but he's not being straight with you," she said earnestly. "He's two-timing you. With Trish, actually!"

"Trish?" Caroline felt a stab of pain. "Are you sure?"

"Oh, yes. When you were at the suppliers this morning, she was boasting that she'll have him all to herself soon. Sorry . . ." Her voice trailed off miserably.

Caroline bit her lip, then tried to speak calmly.

"You were right to tell me, Jan. It can't have been easy for you, but thank you. Now, off you go or you'll miss your bus."

Alone, she sat for a long time at her desk in the back office, staring blankly at the opposite wall with its calendar and sales graphs and company notices, her throat tight with unshed tears.

Only a month ago, she'd stood with Craig watching the New Year's Eve fireworks display by the lake. As the shells burst overhead, showering the sky with chrysanthemums of light, their reflections shimmering in the dark expanse of water, he'd taken her in his arms and kissed her, and she'd known with utter certainty that this was going to be the best year of her life . . .

Caroline heard the mall night-guard rap on the door – it was time he was locking up – and wearily she got to her feet.

As she reached for her shoulder bag, she saw the in-house magazine lying beside it . . .

"SHALL we gift-wrap it for you?" Caroline smiled at her young client.

"That'd be great. I'm terrible with parcels."

"Pink paper, I think, as it's our Wild Rose collection. Would you see to it, please, Noelene?" She slid the small box along the glass counter top to the young assistant.

"Will do, Caro."

"Your grandma will love it, I know," Caroline said, turning back to her customer. "The serum is proving very popular in our stores back in the UK, and I'm sure it'll be just as effective here. You said she has a fair complexion?"

"Yes." The young woman laughed. "English peaches and cream, Grandpa calls it. But it's had a tad too much of our Australian sun since they came out here."

"Well, you've made a great start. And if she likes it, the complementary eye dew and day cream are excellent, too."

"Then just wrap those as well," the girl said impulsively. "She's worth it. She's a darling!"

"I'm sure she is." Caroline smiled warmly. "I sympathise with her – I have the same skin-type." Ruefully she ran a hand through her blonde hair. "I've only been out here two months, but I've learned the hard way what the sun can do. My shoulders got really burned when I was jogging in the park on Tuesday evening."

"But your complexion is great!" the girl exclaimed. "What do you use – if you don't mind me asking?"

"Not at all. I use our Evening Primrose range, actually."

"Well, if it's good enough for you . . ." The girl grinned, brandishing her payment card. "I think I might need a bigger carrier bag!"

"Wow! You're such a great saleswoman," Noelene said when the girl had triumphantly carried off her bulging pink and silver bag.

Caroline laughed.

"Thanks. But you're learning really quickly. In fact –"

She was about to add, "By the time I go back to the UK, mission accomplished, our very first Fliss store established here in Australia, you'll be able to take over." But she thought twice. She didn't want to raise her colleague's hopes yet.

"Just remember what I've said," she went on instead. "Always be yourself. And always be honest. Don't try to sell someone the most expensive line if it won't suit them. They simply won't come back."

The young girl nodded seriously.

"Right, I'll just nip next door to the café for ten minutes while there's a bit of a lull. You can always fetch me if you need me – though I know you'll be fine on your own. Then you can leave a bit early. Didn't you say you've got a new date?"

Noelene nodded shyly.

"A guy called Shane. He's gorgeous!"

Seeing the way the girl's eyes lit up, Caroline winced inwardly. Noelene wasn't much younger than her, but the gap in age seemed light years.

THE café was quiet this late Saturday afternoon, and Caroline chose a table outside under the pergola, from where she could survey the scene around her. The small square near the cathedral was shaded by tall trees and a water feature nearby splashed softly into a basin. Earlier, it had been busy with shoppers, a group doing Tai Chi and a couple of young classical violinists busking, but now it was almost deserted.

Drowsy in the heat, she closed her eyes. Goodness, she was tired – no, exhausted. She'd arrived from a grey Heathrow to dazzling sunshine and to this retail unit, empty apart from the fitted shelves and piles of Fliss-labelled boxes awaiting her.

She had never worked so hard – interviewing potential staff, arranging ads in the local paper, fliers, organising a grand opening with fizz and nibbles and special offers . . . and then crawling off every night to collapse into bed in her tiny flat upstairs. No, she had never worked so hard. Nor, she admitted to herself, had she ever been happier. And if at times she thought of Craig – well, she'd soon get over it, and him.

"Caroline, my dear girl."

She opened her eyes to see Mrs Petrides, the kindly Greek-born café proprietor, bending over her.

"Are you unwell?"

"Oh, no, I'm fine, thank you, Mrs P.," she reassured her quickly. "I'm just tired. And with the sun – I just closed my eyes for a moment. Can I have a pot of tea, please?"

"Of course, my dear."

Mrs Petrides gathered up the empty cups and plates on the next table and carried them away, leaving Caroline idly watching a couple of young cockatoos squabbling in a nearby tree.

"English breakfast tea for an English young lady." Mrs Petrides's son appeared and set a laden tray on the table.

"Oh, hi, Nik! I didn't know you were here."

Nik Petrides was with a big law firm 15 miles away in downtown Sydney, but came back most weekends to help his widowed mother. When Caroline had first met him she'd asked him if he didn't find it too much of a change, but he'd grinned at her.

"Not a bit. I love to get out of my sharp suits and into this," he'd said, gesturing to his barista outfit of black T-shirt and jeans and green apron. "Serving cappuccinos makes a great change from serving writs!"

When he'd got to know her a little better, he'd told her how he would never be able to repay his mother who, widowed young, had worked her fingers to the bone for him and his sister Elena, who was now married with two boys. She had sent them to good schools and had then supported his ambition to go to law school.

In return, Caroline had found herself telling him how she envied him his close-knit family and of her own disrupted upbringing which had left her so insecure.

He'd taken her hand and squeezed it, his brown eyes full of sympathy.

"But you can be proud of your success now, Caroline, and that it is all by your own efforts."

Now, as he set down the white china teapot, he said, "This is on the house," and waved her protests aside. "Mama has told me how you helped her clear up on Tuesday evening when Leanne went home sick."

"It was nothing, really. After all, I only live next door and I could see she was tired."

"And you weren't, I suppose?"

"Well, maybe just a bit." She accepted the tea. "Thank you, Nik."

He glanced round at the empty tables.

"I've told Mama to go off home – there'll be no more customers today. Do you mind if I join you?"

"Of course not. Please do."

She was beginning to like this tough but gentle young man and was glad of the company. He set down a cappuccino, with the café's trademark smiley face etched in chocolate powder on the white froth.

"That face always makes me smile, too," she said, and did so now.

10

He caught her expression.

"That's better. You were looking a bit down."

"Yes, well . . . I was thinking," she said ruefully.

"Not about that undeserving young man in England, I hope?" His tone was only half-teasing.

"Oh, no." To cover her confusion, she occupied herself with the teapot, pouring and adding milk.

There was a companionable silence for a few minutes, then Nik spoke casually.

"Have you made it up to the Blue Mountains yet?"

"No. Noelene keeps telling me I should go, but there's always so much to do."

"Tch." He shook his head reprovingly. "All work and no play . . ."

". . . makes Caroline a dull girl. I know, but I honestly don't have time."

He wasn't taking no for an answer.

"Let's say Wednesday. I'll pick you up early – eight a.m."

TAKE care. It's really slippery." Nik took her hand and Caroline stepped down from rock to rock to the small clearing. "Welcome to the Pool of Siloam."

"Oh, Nik!" Caroline gasped with delight. "It's so beautiful!"

Opposite them a waterfall cascaded down like a bridal veil over the lush ferns growing from the rock face. It fell into a small, shallow pool then trickled away through more ferns.

Impulsively she took off her sandals, waded across the pool and stood letting the spray cool her arms, moist from the afternoon heat. She turned and saw that Nik was holding his camera.

"The beautiful nymph of the spring," he said, and smiled as he showed her the picture on the little screen. Peering at the image he had captured, Caroline saw on her face an expression almost of joy.

Astonished, she looked up at him and what she fleetingly glimpsed in his eyes made her heart flutter – panic close behind it.

"It's really lovely, Nik," she said, drawing back and becoming quite formal. "Thank you for bringing me. I think I could stay here for ever."

"Oh, dear." He laughed and the tension between them was broken. "That's a pity. There's still so much to see, and I've got a table booked for an early dinner."

And with a final backward glance, they began the steep climb back up through the eucalyptus grove.

They had almost reached the summit when, without warning, a wild, crazy laugh broke out just ahead, echoing around them. Caroline flinched and would have stumbled if Nik hadn't caught her up in his arms. She rested there for a moment, so close that she could feel his heart beating, then abruptly she pulled away.

"Sorry." She felt herself colour.

Nik smiled easily.

"Don't worry. It's only a bird – a kookaburra, telling us off. If you've never heard one before, they are a bit unnerving," he added, as the manic laughter died away into silence.

CAROLINE smacked her lips with satisfaction as she put down her dessert spoon.

"Mmm, that lemon mousse was absolutely delicious."

Dusk had fallen while they had been eating and she felt rather than saw his smile across the dinner table. She sat back in her chair and looked around her. The half dozen tables were set on the veranda of the old wooden house, shaded by jasmine whose white flowers gave off a heady perfume.

"This is a lovely place," she said. "A great end to a really great day. I've seen so much – Echo Point, Govett's Leap, that lovely garden with its Art Deco house, and, of course, Siloam. I'm so glad you brought me, Nik."

"And I'm glad you came." He nodded then added quietly, "*Koukla mou.*"

"What does that mean?"

"Oh, it's Greek for –" He broke off and glanced at his watch. "For, it's getting late. You have a shop to open as usual tomorrow, and at half-nine I'm in court."

"Would you like to come in for a coffee?" Caroline asked as Nik's car drew up at the corner of the square.

"Thank you, but no. I have some papers to go through before tomorrow. But –" He hesitated. "Maybe we can do it again some time soon?"

"That would be lovely. And will you be back this weekend?"

"Yes, I'll definitely be back on Saturday."

"Thank you, Nik." She leaned over and impulsively kissed him on the cheek. "It's been wonderful."

She watched the car till it was out of sight, then walked across the square towards the shop.

She was still smiling to herself as she raised her key to unlock the door which led to the flight of stairs up to her flat.

"Hello, Carly." A voice spoke nearby from the darkness.

Carly? Only one person had ever called her that. She dropped the key and spun round.

"Craig? What are you doing here?"

"Waiting for you, Carly. What else? The woman next door said you'd be back about now."

"But . . ." Shock made her all but speechless. "You – you'd better come upstairs."

Once indoors, she gestured him to an armchair.

12

"Sit down. I'll get us something to drink. Coffee?"

"Please." He sat back, quite at ease, looking around him. "This place is nice."

Getting coffees from the kitchen gave her a moment to think, though her thoughts were spinning so fast it was hard to make sense of them.

Back in the living-room, she set down the cups on the table and pushed one towards him.

"Black, no sugar."

"You remembered." He grinned at her. "Stop looking at me as if I'm a ghost."

"It's just, I can hardly believe it. Why are you here? There's nothing wrong at Fliss, is there?"

"Absolutely not – things have never been better. And by the way, congrats. From me, and the girls."

"The girls?"

"Felicity and Lisa, of course. You've done a great job."

"Thank you." She felt a glow of pleasure. "But you haven't come all this way just to tell me that, surely?"

"Well, no. Apart from the pleasure of seeing you, of course, I'm here to suss out a possible location for a second store, this time in Sydney itself. There's a unit come up in the mall where Felicity had her salon all those years ago. You have to give it to those two." He shook his head in admiration. "They've still got their fingers on the pulse."

"But why you, Craig?" Caroline asked faintly. It was an important task for an area manager.

"Well, that'll be because I've been promoted. Actually, they've co-opted me on to the Board."

"Wow! Congratulations. But you've earned it, I'm sure."

"Thanks." He tried to conceal his understandable pride by sounding casual, then went on.

"But that means there's a vacancy for an area manager. And that's where you come in. You've more than proved yourself here. I think you should apply for my old job. You'd make a great area manager."

"You mean at the end of my time here?"

"No, we have to fill the post now. Things are moving fast, Carly. My return flight's in three days' time – and you're booked on it as well."

"Three days? But I can't leave just like that, Craig! I'm interviewing for two more staff on Friday, and . . ."

He waved an airy hand.

"I checked out – what's she called, Noelene – today. She's a bit raw, but the potential's there. She'll cope till we get someone out here next week." He paused, not looking at her. "In fact, Trish is up for it."

"Trish?"

13

He came and sat beside her on the sofa.

"I've been such an idiot, Carly. I've called myself every sort of fool. Trish was just a, well, a moment of madness, and you being out here has shown me that."

He took her hand. She resisted at first, then let it lie.

"So can we start again, darling?"

He gave her that slanting smile that had always made her heart sing, then put his hand to his head.

"Ouch. The jet lag's kicking in, I think. I'd better get back to my hotel."

In her tiny hallway he turned to her, his lips brushing her cheek.

"Goodnight, Carly. Sleep well. I'll collect you at nine tomorrow and we'll head into the city."

From her window, she looked down on him hurrying away across the square. She and Craig were alike in some ways, she thought: both driven by the burning desire to succeed by their own abilities. And this chance he'd given her was what she had striven for. It was within her grasp . . .

She stood for a long time, watching but not seeing, as, one by one, all the lights went out around her.

Saturday morning, she would be at Sydney Airport. Saturday morning, Nik was coming over again . . .

An expectant hush fell across the huge crowd. Then, as one voice, the chant began.

"Ten . . . nine . . . eight . . ." Her heart was beating faster, keeping time. "Three . . . two . . . one."

Then, as the midnight sky erupted in a dazzling crescent of light and sound, she put her hands to her ears. At the same time she felt his arms tighten protectively around her. Laughing, she looked up to see his face, illuminated by the brilliance, filled with tenderness and love.

As she heard the exclamations of Elena and her husband, and their two boys and their grandmother chattering excitedly, unexpected tears glittered in her eyes.

"What's wrong, love?" Nik asked tenderly

She knew what she wanted to say.

"I tried to fool myself, but all my life I've been alone, and now – it's like coming into a bright, warm room from a bitter winter's night."

But somehow she couldn't put it into words, so instead she smiled.

"Nothing – nothing at all." Because in the end, the decision had been easy.

The last fireworks were dying down, the Harbour Bridge dark again.

"Happy New Year, my darling."

"The happiest ever," she whispered, and as the jubilant crowd swirled around them, Nik drew her closer and kissed her. ▪

## The Dandy 1938

**WHAT** child wouldn't have broken into a broad grin to find "The Dandy" among their Christmas parcels? And not just "The Dandy" but the very first "Monster Comic", or annual, as it later became known.

With the familiar face of Korky the Cat on the front cover and old pals such as Desperate Dan and Keyhole Kate inside, many happy hours of reading were assured – even with "hilarious" jokes such as "What is the oldest tree? The elder" gracing many of the pages!

And once the annual was finished, there were other classics published in that year to turn to. Parents or older brothers and sisters might have enjoyed Agatha Christie's latest offering, "Appointment With Death", while children had the treat of T.H. White's "The Sword In The Stone", first in his series "The Once And Future King" and featuring Wart, the young King Arthur, and his (tor)mentor, Merlyn.

Kathleen Hayle's "Orlando (The Marmalade Cat)" also made his first appearance, introducing another character to the world of famous felines, and one who became almost as well-known as Korky himself! ■

# The Buttercup Ring

*by Wendy Clarke.*

TODAY we will have been married 30 years. There will be no cruise, or fancy meal, or cards with rhymes about everlasting love. We have agreed that the car needs a service and, as always, a choice must be made.

I lie beside my husband and watch him as he sleeps. Since giving up on another job, he has got used to sleeping through the alarm. Now he can happily sleep until the morning sun slides through the crack in the curtains and on to his face, causing him to screw up his eyes and pull a pillow over his head.

I, on the other hand, wake with the dawn chorus, after which I tiptoe down to make the tea. Each morning, as the kettle boils, I pull my dressing-gown tighter around me and stand at the window, watching the sky lighten and wondering where the money will come from to pay the council tax or the dentist's bill.

This morning, though, I am in no hurry to get up. I have taken a day's holiday and have promised myself that today, on our anniversary, I shall also give myself a day off from worries. After all, it is hardly the first time in our marriage that we have struggled financially.

Michael flings an arm out across the pillow, lost in a dream. Is it unfair that he worries so little, sailing through life on a sea of smiles?

It is nearly eight and, as the bedroom brightens, the yellow flowers on the duvet cover come into focus, twined together on thin green stems. I am eighteen again and Michael is holding a buttercup under my chin . . .

THE meadow stretches as far as the eye can see – white clover and daisies broken only occasionally by the yellow of a buttercup or the pink starburst of a campion. It's our favourite place. We lie on a tartan rug pulled from the boot of Michael's Mini, and watch the clouds scud across the cobalt blue sky.

"Seems you like butter," he says, tickling my skin with the soft yellow petals.

"Actually no." I laugh. "But then, when have I ever liked what everyone else likes?"

"Nonconformist. I like it."

16

He leans over and kisses me. His eyes become serious.

"Sal, I have something for you."

He sits up and splits the stem of the buttercup with his nail, and I watch as he carefully threads the end of the stem through the gap to make a complete green circle, the butter yellow flower head shining like a jewel.

He takes my hand and pulls me up so that we are sitting knee to knee. His hair flops around a face tanned from long days in the summer sun, and I love the way he is so confident in his own skin.

Holding my hand between his, he slips the flower ring on to my finger.

"I can't afford a proper ring at the moment, Sal. What do you say?"

My heart beats so fast I am sure he must feel it in the pulse of my wrist where his thumb still rests, but even as I hug my happiness to me, I think of the practical things. Where would we live? How would we live? After dropping out of college, Michael has yet to find a job.

"How can we?"

Michael throws himself on to his stomach and picks a blade of grass. Placing the length of it between the soft pads of his thumbs, he raises it to his lips and blows softly, the mournful note cutting through the silence of the meadow.

"How can we not?" he says, turning to me, and I know that he is right.

Yet even in my certainty, for a brief second I see, like a premonition, what our future will hold.

"Are you happy, Sal?" he asks, his eyes searching my face.

I know that the answer is clear.

"Yes, Mike," I say, sweeping the hair from his face. "I'm happy."

"How are you going to live?" my mother asks when we tell her of our plans to marry. "You can't live on love alone."

Our parents and even our friends say that it won't last. We don't care, though; we have no doubts.

Eighteen and in love, we marry in the registry office in town. My dress is from the bridal section of the Oxfam shop where we have also bought Michael's tie, and I carry a bunch of wild columbines from my mother's garden.

Confident in our love, we make our vows then set out to show the world that it is wrong about us.

As the years pass by, jobs come and go. Sometimes it is Michael who loses interest, and sometimes they lose interest in him, but always he just sighs and shrugs.

"Karma," he says, pulling me to him. "There'll be other jobs – you worry too much."

But someone has to.

I take a job at the garden centre – repotting seedlings and watering alpines.

Michael is overjoyed when I tell him I am pregnant, but as my belly swells and our precious baby grows inside me, I wonder how we will manage when I have to give up work.

Michael has joined an agency and takes jobs when he is offered them, but all too often I recognise the look in his eyes that tells me that soon, for one reason or another, the job will come to an end.

When Cara is born, Michael looks at her as though she is the most wondrous thing he has seen. He holds her tiny hand to his lips and whispers secrets to her, and, as she grows, he sits with her in the tiny scrap of garden behind the house and tells her stories.

This is where I often find them when I come home from work, sitting on the grass with a picture book between them, strings of daisies around their necks . . .

NOW, as the sunlight streaks a zigzag across his face, Michael stirs. He flings an arm across his eyes and groans, the morning light catching the grey flecks in his hair.

"Is it morning already?"

"Yes, it's morning."

"You haven't got up yet?"

I stroke the golden hairs on his arms.

"No, not yet."

He turns to me.

"Happy anniversary, Sal. I would make the tea but I didn't get to bed till late. Would you mind?"

He will be tired after staying up late to e-mail Cara – he must have crept into bed long after I was asleep. I know that he misses her. We both do.

I throw off the duvet and search for my dressing-gown, but stop as Michael links my wrist with his fingers.

"Are you happy, Sal?" He squints up at me through the sandy sweep of his eyelashes.

This is the question he asks me every anniversary and I know that my answer is as important to him now as it ever was.

The wooden boards are cold under my feet as I make my way downstairs. Two years ago we ripped up the old stair carpet, but another job loss meant no money to replace it.

On the doormat below the letter-box lies a card. I smile, knowing it is from Cara. It will be the only card we will receive today.

*To Mum and Dad*, I read. *Thirty years! You may be chalk and cheese but you were made for each other.*

I touch a hand to my throat and blink away the tears that are threatening to fall. Is it so obvious?

The kitchen door is ajar and I nudge it open with my shoulder, Cara's words turning in my head. I stop in the doorway and stare, not sure if maybe I am still dreaming. Every surface has been filled with wild flowers: arching stems of willowherb share vases with twisting bindweed and small purple cushions of knapweed.

On the table, an old water jug, a long-forgotten wedding present, overflows with pink and red campion, while the window-sill is a festival of pinks, purples, blues and yellows. Through the archway that leads to the living-room I see still more flowers.

"And this is for you, Sal," a soft voice behind me says.

Michael rests his hands on my shoulders and slowly turns me around. He lifts my hand and places on my finger, above my wedding band, a perfect buttercup ring.

"For my girl who hates butter," he says.

I look at this man and see again a meadow full of flowers and that young boy with his head in the clouds. I knew who he was then and I am glad that he is still that person. The yin to my yang.

"You never answered my question, Sal."

"Yes, Mike. I'm happy. I'm very happy."

And I know that, despite everything, and against the odds, it is the truth. ▦

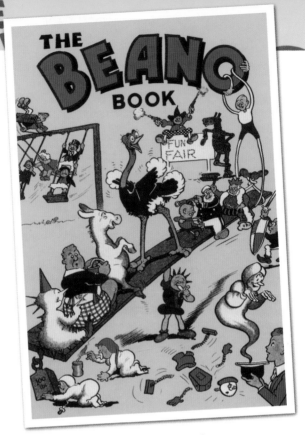

## The Beano 1940

**IT'S** over 75 years since "The Beano" first became a playground staple. Lord Snooty and his Pals, Big Eggo, Pansy Potter The Strong Man's Daughter and others were destined to become firm favourites, and all made an appearance in "The Beano Book", first published in 1940.

Children at the time had reason to be glad of the treats afforded by their comics, as this was the year that food rationing began in Britain, sweets in particular being in short supply.

It was a grim year for all, as war had begun, and with it the onset of the Blitz at the end of the year. The release of Walt Disney's "Fantasia" and "Pinocchio" helped to dispel the gloom, and Charlie Chaplin's "The Great Dictator" gave cinemagoers welcome light relief from serious concerns. British entertainers did their bit as Arthur Askey brought audiences to tears of a happy kind in "Charley's Aunt". Children were not forgotten, either, as Richmal Compton's ever-popular William Brown appeared on the big screen in "Just William".

But it was the everyday joy of comics that kept on coming week after week, and many a child would have been thrilled to receive their first "Beano" annual to cheer the end of a challenging year. ∎

*Illustration by Majken Thorsen.*

# The Bandsman

### *by Mary Kettlewell.*

FAINT on the winter's afternoon came the sound of a brass band. Kath pulled the blue scarf up over her head and huddled deep into her winter coat against the biting wind. She stepped carefully along the icy pavement, drawn by the sound of trombones and the rumble of drums.

Rounding the corner by Woolworths, she stopped dead in her tracks, eyes fixed. Surely that bandsman blowing the cornet was Ken! Her heart raced as she took in the familiar dark-blue coat and pressed trousers, the peaked cap and black shoes.

He half turned and smiled, and disappointment coursed through her frame. It was a stranger. Of course it was. She railed inwardly at her

21

foolishness. Ken was two thousand miles away, in Cyprus with the British Army, trying to bring about peace between the Turkish and Greek communities.

Kath remained there, deep in thought, unaware of the damp and cold creeping up through the soles of her boots, the whirl of snowflakes in the bitter air and the strains of "In The Bleak Midwinter".

\* \* \* \*

It was during her first week as a cook at the headquarters of the Royal Military School of Music that she had first set eyes on Ken. A group of trainee musicians was practising a march. Some wore bearskins, red jackets and neatly ironed trousers. Others sported peaked caps with scarlet ribbons and white webbing over their uniforms.

She watched as the warrant officer raised his baton for "The British Grenadiers". Just then one of the trombonists hit a wrong note.

"Wakey, wakey, trombones!" he barked. "You sound like a group of mewling cats!" He dismissed the men.

Kath's high cheekbones, thick brown hair and generous mouth clearly had not been lost on one of the brass players. He came across, grinning.

"You must think we're a band of no-hopers."

"It was really good . . . until the last bit!"

He looked at her appraisingly.

"I've not seen you here before."

"It's my first week. I'm one of the civilian cooks. Kath Sledmere."

"Ken Brown. I've just started this music training course."

"I'm not very good at identifying musical instruments. What is it you were playing?"

"A cornet. I'm learning to be a bugler, as well."

"What job do buglers do in the Army, then?"

"What job?" He laughed. "We only keep it from falling apart! We call reveille at six o'clock in the morning to a volley of curses from the lads, who think it's the middle of the night!"

Kath smiled.

"I've read somewhere you bugle them to meals."

"We do. That makes us a bit more popular. 'Come To The Cookhouse Door, Boys'. I expect you know the tune?" He whistled it and she nodded.

"Listen, I've got a thirty-six-hour pass on Saturday. Do you fancy coming for a drink? I know a nice pub overlooking the Thames."

"OK. I'll try to wangle the afternoon off. One of my friends owes me a favour."

Kath had taken to the young man at first sight, what with his smart uniform, sense of humour and liking for music.

The following Saturday they were sitting on a terrace with the water

22

lapping at the wooden stanchions below. A pleasure boat went by and a group of schoolchildren waved.

"What made you join up in the Army, Ken?"

"I had a boring job welding car parts in a factory, and I love music. I've always fancied playing in a brass band. So I signed on for three years and applied for this course. What about you?"

"I did a domestic science certificate at college, and I wanted a job in central London. Helping in Mum and Dad's paper shop was driving me bonkers."

They chatted away, stared at by a fierce-looking pair of swans, and Kath felt as if she was sharing the afternoon with an old friend.

They agreed to meet to feed the ducks in St James Park and listen to the concert at the bandstand the following Saturday.

✳ ✳ ✳ ✳

A woman's voice brought her back to the present with a jolt.

"You'll be frozen stiff, love. You've been standing there all of forty minutes in the cold!"

Kath found herself looking into the friendly eyes of a late-middle-aged member of the band who was holding a flugelhorn.

"Sorry. I was miles away."

The woman gave her a long stare.

"Are you feeling all right? You look a bit upset."

Kath could only shrug miserably.

"Come into the hall for a cup of tea and a chinwag," the woman urged. "It's better to get things off your chest. My name's Maggie Foreman. I've three girls of my own, grown up now and living up north. So I'm an old hand at listening!"

She settled Kath at a table and came back with mugs of tea and currant buns. Then she glanced down at Kath's ring finger, where the golden band shone brightly.

"Not been married long, then?"

"Just six months ago. At St Jude's church." Kath took a long sip of tea and felt her eyes misting over. "My husband's off on a Cyprus posting. I haven't seen him for over three months."

"A soldier? That's hard on a young wife. You'll be worried about him."

"It's all this trouble with that Archbishop Makarios. I'm so afraid something will happen to him."

Maggie added a spoonful of sugar to her cup.

"Things are calming down now. I read in today's 'Gazette' that the prime ministers of Turkey and Greece, and our Mr Harold Macmillan, are holding talks to bring about peace. They'll be sending all our lads home soon, if you ask me."

Kath dabbed at her eyes.

▶

▶ "You think he'll be all right?"

"Hope for the best in life and you often find it'll happen. Now, tell me all about your fellow."

"He's an Army musician. He plays the cornet and he's one of the camp buglers as well." She smiled through her tears. "He wrote and told me the Army in Cyprus would collapse without him, because he gives the waking-up calls, the bedtime blast and summons them to meals!"

Maggie laughed.

"Think positive, and keep your chin up. I'm sure that's what he would want."

"Thank you for being so kind, Mrs Foreman. It's cheered me up."

"My pleasure. And we're here every weekend if you're feeling a bit lonely."

A LETTER was waiting for Kath back home. It had an Army clearance stamp on it. She picked it up, her hands shaking with excitement.

*Darling Kath,*

*I'm missing you something awful. It feels as if we are living in different worlds, it being warm and sunny here and you with snow and ice. I can't say much, because of security, but things are looking up and the CSM said the top brass were talking about peace. Roll on home time, sweetheart.*

*The music has kept all our spirits up. Last week we laid on a concert for the camp and I had to play the French horn because the usual lad was off sick. We did old favourites to remind us of home, like "Rule Britannia" and "Men Of Harlech". We got three encores! Colonel Fawcett said our playing was important because it raised the morale of the men. It was like a glue binding soldiers together.*

*I'm hoping against hope that we'll soon be packing up our kitbags and setting off home. I can't wait. Kisses and hugs enough to fill a million mess tins,*

*Your Ken.*

*PS Do you remember our stupid quarrel on Hampstead Heath before I left? Making up afterwards was the best thing ever. I'll never forget all those cuddles.*

Kath cooked herself sausages and chips and sat at the table reading and re-reading Ken's letter. It had been early spring when they'd caught the bus to Hampstead Heath. They had walked through the grass hand in hand watching a herd of shy deer graze and fade away into the bushes. Later they had fish and chips and glasses of ale in a pub.

Ken looked at his watch.

"What time did you say the last bus goes back to Twickenham?"

"Ten fifty. I checked on the timetable before we left."

They went to the bus stop. An old man walking his dog called out to them.

"You've missed the last bus. It went half an hour ago."

## Glen Lyon

ALL January the hills curved with perfect snow;
Now this morning the grazed eyeball of a moon
Rolls into the blue silence. A sunlight,
Frail and liquid, sluices all the fields.

A tattered huddle of a lamb
Rends the day with sadness.
The trees whisper, lift and fall;
There flutters on the breeze sleet, soft as wool.

*– Kenneth Steven.*

"I thought you said it left at ten fifty?" Ken had snapped at her.
"Don't blame me! It's what the timetable says."
"Where? Let's have a look." He peered at it and frowned angrily. "This expired at the end of March, for heaven's sake!"
"That's not my fault. It's what they gave me in the bus station!"
"Now what are we going to do? You'll get me put on a charge."
"I know what I'm going to do," she replied thinly. "Get a taxi. You please yourself!" She flagged one down, and through the window saw him storming off in the opposite direction.
That night she cried herself to sleep, thinking that it was all over, not realising that lovers' quarrels came and went as quickly as summer rain. Ken was waiting outside the kitchen door when her shift ended, with a

▶

▶ huge bunch of flowers, a sheepish face and words of apology.

"I'm sorry, Kath. I didn't mean any of what I said. I love you to bits."

"It was my fault as much as yours, Ken," she said, putting her arms round him. "I thought you wouldn't want to see me again!"

"Kath, I've been awake half the night wishing I could take back my words. You couldn't be more wrong. There's something I want to ask. I've got a ring in my pocket. Please will you let me put it on your finger?"

Afterwards he took her in his arms and the world faded away and she had never known such happiness and joy.

THE band was in the same place outside Woolworths the following week. Maggie took the flugelhorn from her mouth and waved cheerfully. Well wrapped up, Kath listened, a touch sad as the snowflakes drifted down and her breath frosted in the icy air. She thought of Ken blowing the bugle for reveille as the sun rose in the eastern Mediterranean, of him standing outside the dining hall in his uniform, calling the men to lunch.

She relived that long, lingering embrace they had shared before the troop ship pulled away from its moorings, taking her new husband with it. She had not known it was possible to feel so wretched . . .

The band packed away its instruments and Kath felt a hand on her shoulder.

"Did you hear our last one, dear?" Maggie asked. "It was 'Bravest Of The Brave'. I chose it especially for your Ken. We owe those lads a lot for risking their lives. Come and have a mug of tea. You never finished telling me about your wedding."

\*   \*   \*   \*

Two months later the Treaty of Zurich was signed, granting Cyprus independence, and the first British contingent prepared to come home.

Shortly afterwards a letter dropped through Kath's letterbox.

*Darling,*

*I'm sure you've heard the wonderful news. The fighting is at an end and we're shortly due to board the ship for England. God willing, I'll be with you in a fortnight. Your ever-loving Ken.*

She rushed along to tell Maggie on the next Saturday, the letter fluttering in her hand.

"You've been a real brick, Maggie. I'd never have got by without you keeping me cheerful."

"Nonsense, Kath. You're a strong woman, or you wouldn't have been able to cope so well all these months without him. Anyway, I miss my girls, and having you close by is like having another daughter."

Kath's eyes misted over and she swallowed hard.

"That's a lovely thing to say," she said quietly. "Did I tell you there's going

26

to be a welcome-home parade for the troops, according to rumours at the music school!"

"It'll be the happiest day of your life, love, apart from that wedding day you told me about!"

POLICE held back the crowds and they all waited – wives, children, mothers, aunts, cousins, grannies and grandads – for their loved ones to arrive. In the distance they could hear the thud of boots, and then the strains of a brass band.

Suddenly, there was Ken, suntanned now, a touch thinner and as handsome as ever.

As he marched past playing the cornet he stole her a loving look, and her heart nearly burst with pride. She had to wait half an hour before he was free to take her in his arms, in the town hall.

"Ken, you're back!"

She buried her head in his tunic and he stroked back the hair from her face tenderly. And there, in that crowded hall, his lips closed on hers and all her longings of the last six months were met in that precious moment.

That night, as they sat before the fire, he told her of his plans.

"I've bought myself out of the Forces, Kath. I can't bear being apart from you."

She couldn't take in the news at first.

"You mean you are leaving the Army?"

"Yes. I've been offered a civilian job at the school of music, teaching the bugle to new recruits."

She jumped up from her chair.

"Oh, Ken, we'll be able to settle down and have our own home!"

"And a family," he added. "Not to mention a wonderful cook for a wife, who can help me forget those greasy cookhouse meals we ate abroad."

\*  \*  \*  \*

Kath introduced Ken to Maggie. They took her out to a Golden Egg restaurant, to tell her the good news and to thank her for what she had done.

"I am so grateful to you for looking out for Kath," Ken said earnestly.

"It was nothing, Ken," Maggie protested, flushing. "The poor girl was half freezing in the snow, thinking and fretting about you so far away in Cyprus. All I gave her was a cup of hot, sweet tea."

"And hope, and sympathy, and reassurance," Kath added, giving a fond look to this kind woman, who had befriended her when she was at such a low point. "Ken, darling, do you remember what Colonel Fawcett said to you? Music is like glue. It sticks people together. You and me, and Maggie!"

"That's all very well," her friend replied briskly, "but I'd best be off, or the concert this evening will go ahead minus one flugelhorn player!" ■

## Lochgoilhead, Argyll

SITUATED within Loch Lomond and the Trossachs National Park, Lochgoilhead is an ideal base for exploring the beautiful west coast of Scotland. It's off the beaten track, yet still easily accessible, just 90 minutes by road from Glasgow city centre or Oban.

Loch Lomond and the Trossachs National Park is the fourth largest park in the UK and includes 21 Munros. For walkers seeking a challenge, the West Highland Way passes through the park, while the mountains of Ben Lomond and the Cobbler in the Arrochar Alps attract most hikers.

Lochgoilhead is surrounded by mountains, some of them as high as 3,000 feet, and is situated at the head of Loch Goil. If you're a fisherman, you might be interested to know that there are several Scottish sea fishing shore records attributed to the loch.

You might even recognise this small village if you are a James Bond fan, as it featured in the 1963 film "From Russia With Love" when Sean Connery shot two villains in a helicopter!

Lochgoilhead might be small, but thanks to tourism the village population more than doubles during the summer months. Don't expect a motorway or even a dual carriageway, though, as two single-track roads lead both in and out of this village. ■

*Illustration by Andy Walker.*

# Ollie's Choice

## — *by Sarah Purdue.* —

OLLIE has wanted a dog for as long as I can remember. The word "dog" has appeared on every Christmas and birthday list since he learned to speak. Dan and I always tried to explain the reasons why we couldn't have a dog, secretly hoping it was a phase that Ollie would grow out of.

When I pick up the crumpled-up piece of paper from the mess that covers Ollie's bedroom carpet I know that we have been foolish ever to think that. Ollie is going to be nine years old in a month's time and at the

29

top of his list for his ninth birthday is *dog*. Only this time it has been scribbled out. Not, I suspect, because he has changed his mind, but because he knows that we will find any number of reasons as to why we can't have one.

As I make supper that night for Dan and myself I think about all those reasons we have previously come up with. The first was that the house and garden were too small. But we moved last year to a new house and now have a large garden. The second reason was that we didn't think Ollie was mature enough to care for a dog, but I know that isn't true any more, either. Last year was really tough, with the loss of Ollie's beloved grandpa and the move so we could be nearer Dan's mother, Cathy. Ollie had to change schools and leave all his friends behind, and he never once complained. Maybe it is time to reconsider?

"Ollie's birthday," I say to Dan later whilst he pours us each a glass of wine. "I was wondering about what we should get him as a present."

Dan sets the plates of food down on the table.

"A new bike? His one seems like it's getting a bit small for him."

"I was thinking more along the lines of something we know he has always wanted."

Dan sighs and I know that he knows exactly what I am talking about.

"He's been so great this year, and has really grown up a lot, Dan."

He runs a hand through his hair, a sure sign that he is giving it some serious thought.

"I know. But what if the novelty wears off after a couple of weeks and we end up lumbered with it for years to come?"

I laugh.

"I don't think that's going to happen. Besides, I found this in his room."

I hand him the piece of paper.

Dan studies the list and I let him think for a few minutes.

"I think we could manage, you know. And I think it would be good for him. He's been pretty quiet lately."

Dan nods.

"I've been worried about him. I'd like to have the old Ollie back – see him laugh, be a kid again."

The frown clears from his face and he lifts his glass into the air.

"To the new member of the family!"

THREE weeks later I am not sure who is more excited, Ollie or me. I can't wait to see his face when he opens his present. I can see mixed emotions on Dan's face. He is clearly still a little unsure that he is ready for a furry addition to the family.

Ollie works to tear off the wrapping paper and is left with a plain brown box. I can see confusion on his face.

"Open it, sweetheart," I say encouragingly.

Ollie slips a finger under the sticky tape holding down the lid and his eyes grow wide with hope as he pulls out a bright-red dog lead.

"Really?" he asks.

I nod and he launches himself into my arms.

"Where is he?" Ollie shouts, practically shaking with excitement.

Dan smiles.

"You didn't think that we would pick a dog without you, did you?"

Ollie throws himself into his dad's arms.

"Thank you, thank you, thank you!"

"Go and get dressed, tiger. We have to find you a dog!"

Ollie pauses.

"Is Granny coming?" he asks with a serious look on his face.

"Of course. She wouldn't want to miss that!" I smile reassuringly at him.

His granny has been withdrawn, and I know that Ollie has noticed. It is difficult to explain to him that putting your life back together after such a loss takes time. I look at Dan and swallow down the lump in my throat.

"Right decision?" I ask with a sly smile.

"You were right, as always." He gives me a peck on the cheek. "Just remember, no big dogs. We want one of a nice manageable size." Dan shows me with his hands the size of his ideal dog.

THE dog shelter is full to bursting point, a sad reflection of it being six weeks after Christmas, the helper, Sue, tells us. Ollie goes from cage to cage, studying each one carefully. Finally he gets to the last cage.

"Well?" I ask.

Ollie puts his hand to his chin and looks the very image of his beloved grandpa trying to make an important decision. Cathy gives a watery smile when I catch her eye. Dan, too.

Without saying a word Ollie makes his way back up the row of cages. He stops in front of one which houses the biggest dog I have ever seen. I can feel the anxiety rolling off Dan, since this dog by no means fits his criteria of a "sensible" size.

Ollie turns and beckons his granny forward. She joins him at his side.

"Honey," I suggest carefully, "don't you think he's a little large for you?"

Ollie turns and looks at me as if I have gone completely mad.

"No," he says. "He's perfect."

I try not to sigh. I desperately want to give him what he wants, but even I am not sure we have room for a dog that could be mistaken for a small pony! Only then do I realise that Ollie has his eyes fixed on the next cage.

Sue hurries over.

"Oh, I don't think you want that one, honey," she says in a voice best suited to toddlers. Fortunately Ollie was raised to be polite, so he gives her his best smile.

"Yes, I do, thank you."

Dan is staring inside the cage, and I know that we are thinking the same thing. Crouching in one corner and shivering so hard that I can see it from the other side of the cage, all we can make out is a bundle of fur.

"Can I go in and meet him?" Ollie asks, hopping from foot to foot.

"No, I'm afraid not. He isn't suitable for adoption. Sometimes dogs are so frightened that they can lash out," Sue says.

Ollie looks quizzical.

"It means he might bite you, sweetheart," his granny says with a look of concern.

I sigh. I desperately want to give Ollie what he wants this time round.

"He's been like that since he came in," Sue says sadly. "He was found abandoned and he hasn't coped well with kennels."

"He won't bite me. He just needs someone who he can trust to look after him," Ollie says firmly and kneels down by the cage.

He puts two fingers through the bars and his granny, with one eye on the pitiful creature in the corner, reaches out gently to pull him back.

But then she stops. I can see that my mother-in-law is studying the poor mite who is standing on shaky legs and moving warily towards Ollie.

"Ollie," Dan says with a clear warning tone.

I keep my eyes fixed on the dog, whose huge brown eyes are fixed on my son.

"It's all right, Daniel, I don't think he is going to bite," Cathy says.

I try to tame the curl of fear in my stomach. I can't imagine a worse way to celebrate Ollie's birthday than a trip to the Accident & Emergency department to get patched up following a dog bite.

NOW I'm closer I can see that the dog is some sort of spaniel mix with floppy ears. I watch, holding my breath, as it makes a slow, ginger path towards Ollie.

"It's OK, boy, I'm not going to hurt you," Ollie tells the animal in a quiet voice.

Gently, the dog starts to lick at Ollie's fingers. Then there is the merest wiggle from his tail end, and I realise that he is starting to wag his tail.

"See, I told you!" Ollie says. "He won't hurt me. He just needs someone to look after him."

Ollie's granny gives his shoulder a squeeze, and then she slowly holds out her hand so that the dog can sniff her, too.

I look behind me at Sue, the helper. She is looking on with amazement.

"Could we at least try?" I suggest. "If we are very careful and take things really slowly . . . It does seem, doesn't it, that they like each other?"

Sue looks again from the abandoned animal to the serious little boy, and seems to make up her mind.

"I'll go and fetch Sandy. She is our behaviour expert, so she'll have a better idea than I do."

S ANDY has put the dog on his lead, and we remain at a safe distance whilst we walk out to the enclosed grass exercise space. Only once Sandy is happy that the dog is calm does she call Ollie over.

"Come forward quietly, now, Ollie. I'm going to keep a close hold on him."

Ollie does as he's instructed. I reach for Dan's hand and squeeze it furiously. I almost can't bear to look. I so desperately want this to work out, but it's not just for Ollie. It's also for the little dog, who I know will fit in perfectly with the family.

He even passes my husband's size restrictions.

Ollie's granny is smiling, as if she knows something we don't.

"Hello, boy," Ollie says and carefully lays a hand on the dog's head.

The animal in turn gently sniffs at Ollie, before rolling on to his back and showing off his soft downy belly.

Sandy looks up.

"I think we have our answer. We'll need to do some work with him, though, Ollie, before we can be sure he will be OK to come home with you."

My son nods, but he only has eyes for the little dog, who is now reaching up and licking his nose. Then there is that magical noise that I have missed so much – the sound of Ollie laughing.

Sandy hands him a ball, and he stands up, throwing it away from him. The dog lurches forward, with Ollie in fast pursuit.

"Granny, come here and meet Billy!" he calls.

I reach for my mother-in-law's hand, hearing her gasp, and give it a squeeze.

I remember the story, too, the one that my dear father-in-law used to tell. About his first dog, Billy, who he found wandering in the street when he was a young boy, and who he had taken home and loved.

Beside me, I can see a silent tear roll down Cathy's cheek.

"Watch this, Granny!" Ollie shouts as he throws a ball high in the air and Billy leaps up to catch it. "Isn't he clever?"

Cathy smiles and nods.

"He's just perfect, Ollie. A great choice."

She walks over and picks up the ball before throwing it across the grass, laughing as Billy and Ollie race to get to it first. I feel Dan's arm around me, and I know that everything is going to be OK, both for us and for the newest addition to our family. ■

# When The Snowdrops Bloom

### by Pat Posner.

EBRUARY is such a dreary month!" Anita shivered as she walked into the kitchen.

Her mum nodded.

"It's the coldest one I've known since we came to live here. And I haven't got the living-room fire going yet. Not that it would make much difference. That's the downside of prefabs – they're almost impossible to keep warm in this weather.

"Tell you what, love," she added, "I'll light the gas oven and leave the door open and we'll eat in here. I've made porridge."

Anita pulled the ironing board down from the wall so they could use it as a table, then, smiling, went to get a couple of chairs. It was a good job her dad wasn't home from working his night shift yet, as he wouldn't approve of eating off the ironing board, nor of using the gas oven to keep them warm. Bit of a stickler for things like that, was Dad.

"This is probably the only chance I'll have of eating anything until this evening," Anita said as she sprinkled sugar on her porridge. "It'll be extra busy at work today, with everyone wanting a shampoo and set so they look good for the Valentine's Day dances."

"I hope you're going to one, too?"

Anita shook her head and concentrated on eating. With Michael away doing his National Service, dressing up and making herself look attractive would feel like she was being disloyal to him. She'd explained this many times before to her mum, and she didn't want to get involved in that sort of conversation again.

Her mum obviously had no such qualms, though, because she sighed loudly.

"Doesn't seem right to me, you staying home on a Saturday night at your age."

"It wouldn't seem right going to a Valentine's Day dance without Michael, either! Besides, I won't be staying at home; I'm babysitting for Richard and

*Illustration by David Young.*

Josie so they can go out."

"That's no different. You'll still be stuck indoors on your own, instead of out enjoying yourself."

Anita shrugged. Josie had been one of her first customers at the hairdressing salon. They'd got on well and had soon become good friends. Richard was nice, too, and Anita enjoyed going round to their place.

"They've got a television, you know, Mum. So I'll be doing something a lot of others round here can't do – watching 'Saturday Night At The London Palladium'!" She stood up to take her empty pots to the sink. And hopefully, she added silently, she'd have a Valentine's card from Michael to keep her company.

It wouldn't be long before she knew. She almost always saw Robert the postman on her way to the bus stop.

As she opened the garden gate, Anita stopped a moment to glance at the snowdrops which, in spite of the frozen earth, were making a brave show beneath the leafless lilac tree.

This was the third year they'd bloomed. The first time had been on February 13, 1952, almost two years ago to the day.

Anita remembered it clearly. It was the day before Michael had left. He'd kissed her goodbye at the gate and afterwards she'd pointed to the flowers and quoted lines from a poem written by the Victorian poet Annie Matheson.

"Two little snowdrops, in green and white,
rose out of the darkness and into the light;
and softly kissed one another."

Remembering that kiss was bittersweet. It had been so special, yet it also made her miss Michael all the more. But it wouldn't be too long now before he came back.

She could see Robert up ahead and, trying not to slip on the icy pavement, she quickened her step. She felt sure he'd have something for her. He was Michael's brother, and for her twenty-first birthday last year Michael had posted cards for her to Robert way ahead of time and had asked Robert to deliver them on the right day.

Robert looked grim as he stood waiting for her. Probably frozen to the marrow, she thought.

"Nice weather if you're a polar bear!" she greeted him jokingly.

His face didn't crack as he handed her an envelope.

"It's a card," he said. "But it isn't from our Michael."

"You do have a card or letter for me from Michael, though?"

Robert shook his head.

She looked closely at him, trying to see if he was having her on.

"Oh, I get it," she said. "It isn't Valentine's Day until tomorrow. You're coming round with it tomorrow, is that it?"

"Sorry, Anita. Michael hasn't sent me anything. You've got a card from somebody, though, haven't you? Sealed with a loving kiss as well!" He jabbed a gloved hand at the card he'd given her, which had the letters *SWALK* on the envelope.

Anita frowned and ripped the envelope open. Inside was a card, all satin and cobwebby lace.

"It's from *A Secret Admirer*," she read, frowning. "Oh, I recognise this handwriting – it's my boss's son. He's only eighteen and he knows I'm spoken for. At least, I think I am," she added wistfully, worried she'd cry if she said any more.

Robert touched her arm lightly.

"Michael might have sent something to me to give you and it's been delayed. It has got to be better getting it a day or two late than not at all, hasn't it?"

The words didn't bring her much comfort as she walked towards the bus stop. She hadn't heard from Michael since Christmas. He wasn't good at writing regularly, but there wasn't usually a six-week gap between letters. And when he did write, his letters were friendly but not exactly romantic. She worried sometimes that Michael wasn't as serious about her as she was about him.

**W**HAT'S up, Anita? You haven't gone and cut my hair wrong, have you?"

Anita smiled at her last customer of the day and shook her head.

"Your hair is going to look lovely, Maureen. But I feel like someone's blown my ankles up with a bicycle pump. I've been on my feet for over eight hours without a seat."

"You'll have to stick them in warm water and mustard when you get home, else you'll not be fit for going dancing tonight. Where are you going? The Valentine's Day dance at the Salford Palais is always good."

"I'm babysitting for friends so they can go dancing," Anita said. "They've got a television set so I'll be watching a variety show or a play."

Gosh, she'd said that so many times today she must sound like a record that had got stuck.

"Your boyfriend keeping you company, is he?" Maureen asked with a cheeky smile.

"Michael's still doing his National Service. Last time he wrote he said he'd be home before Easter, so it won't be that long before I see him again."

"It's a long time to spend away from each other," Maureen commented. "I couldn't stop wondering if my Roy would still want to be my boyfriend when he came out. You do worry about things like that, don't you?"

Anita sighed and nodded.

"Feelings can change when you're not together," Maureen continued.

Anita wasn't sure if Maureen was making her feel better or worse.

"Awful at writing, Roy was," Maureen continued. "Managed to send me a couple of lovely Valentine's Day cards, though. I know you aren't supposed to, but he put his name on them, bless him. Everything turned out all right for me and Roy in the end. Did you get a Valentine's Day card from your Michael, Anita?"

Anita quickly reached for the hand mirror to show Maureen the back of her hair. As she'd hoped, Maureen was so busy admiring her new hairstyle that she didn't say another word about boyfriends or Valentine's cards.

But, silly or not, Anita decided there and then she'd take last year's Valentine's card from Michael with her tonight, to dream over while she was babysitting.

✳  ✳  ✳  ✳

"Was the baby good for you, Anita?" her mum asked at breakfast the next morning.

Dad was home today so they were eating at the proper table. He must have got up early and lit the fire, Anita thought. It was burning away merrily and, although there had been ice on the inside of the bedroom and bathroom windows, it felt quite warm here in the living-room.

"She was as good as gold, Mum. I gave her a bottle at ten o'clock, and she went straight to sleep when I put her back in her cot."

"Did you enjoy the television programmes, Anita?" her dad asked.

Anita hid a smile when she felt her mum kicking her lightly under the table. She knew Mum wanted her to answer enthusiastically. Mum had been trying to persuade Dad to get a television set for months.

"Oh, I did, Dad!" Anita replied. "'Saturday Night At The London Palladium' had some lovely performers on, and then there was a Scotland Yard case history. That was really good."

"Did Josie and Richard enjoy the dance?"

"They did. But they're home-birds really, Mum. Just happy being together in their lovely little house."

Anita loved her job as a hairdresser, but she always felt a bit jealous when she saw Richard and Josie's contentment. It was what she dreamed of for her and Michael one day.

Maureen's words from yesterday kept playing in her head.

"Feelings can change when you're not together." That's what she'd said. And seeing how Michael hadn't written for weeks and it seemed, too, that he hadn't sent her a Valentine's card, maybe his feelings had changed.

"I don't want another cuppa, thanks, Mum. I think I'll read my 'Hairdressers Journal'. Got to keep up with all the latest hairstyles and products."

Once in her bedroom, Anita lay on her bed and continued to brood. It wasn't like her to feel like this. Oh, she missed Michael all the time, but she usually thought happy thoughts of how it would be when he came home. That's what she should be doing now, she told herself crossly.

She hadn't meant to fall asleep, but realised she must have done when she became aware of a voice from the wireless in the living-room.

"The time in Britain is twelve noon, in Germany it's one o'clock, but home and away, it's time for 'Two-Way Family Favourites'."

It was a ritual for the three of them to listen to the programme together. Anita jumped off the bed and arrived in the living-room just as the signature tune was ending.

## Spring In The Air

THERE'S a spring in my step now that
  spring's in the air,
The barometer's needle points steadfastly "Fair",
The fronds of the willow reflecting the sheen,
Decidedly showing a tinting of green.
Soon martins and swallows will take to the sky,
As tirelessly toing and froing they fly.
Lambs in the pasture will bleat, newly born,
By the fresh, dewy glistening daisy-clad lawn.
Blackbirds and thrushes their duets will sing,
To joyously welcome another new spring . . .

*– Brian H. Gent.*

Seeing Mum and Dad sitting in their armchairs either side of the fire, Mum's knitting-needles clicking quietly and the aroma of Erinmore from Dad's pipe, brought the yearning feeling back again. Would her dreams for her and Michael ever come true?

Anita settled down on the sofa, only half-listening to the messages to and from loved ones and the songs they'd requested. It came as somewhat of a shock suddenly to hear her own name, and a song request for her from Michael! She was aware of Mum letting her knitting drop into her lap and Dad putting his pipe on the hearth and turning the wireless up as Bing Crosby sang "May I?" especially for her!

"It's a proposal, Anita," her mum said. "Michael's saying what he feels for you. He wants to hear you say 'I do'. Oh, Anita, isn't it romantic?"

"I, I . . ." Anita couldn't say any more; she just let her tears flow.

"Silly goose," her dad said gruffly as he got up from his chair and stepped over to her, holding out a white handkerchief.

Smiling, Anita mopped her tears.

"This was the best Sunday dinner ever," Anita said later. Her dad had brought a large bottle of lemonade home from the Woodman's and made them all a martini and lemonade to drink with their meal, because it was a special occasion.

"It's a shame we've got to do something as mundane as washing the pots," her mum said, laughing.

Anita collected the used plates together and stood, ready to take them through to the kitchen. Before she had time to move there was a rapping at the front door.

"I'll go," she said. "It'll be another neighbour come to ask me if I heard my name on the wireless."

Smiling, Anita walked into the hall. When she opened the door she gasped and blinked.

"Michael! I can't believe it's really you!"

"Anita?" He sounded shy and uncertain. "Did you hear it?"

Half-crying, half-laughing, she moved towards him and sighed happily as his arms went round her and pulled her close.

"Did Robert know you'd be here for Valentine's Day?"

"He knew I'd be here either today or tomorrow. He said he felt awful that he couldn't even drop you a hint, Anita. But I'd sworn him to secrecy."

Anita sniffed against his shoulder.

"I was upset not to get a card from you."

"I wanted to bring myself instead of sending a card," he murmured into her ear. "I could never seem to write the words to tell you how much I missed you, how much I loved you. That's why I didn't write very often. But I loved you more every day, even though we were apart."

He moved back slightly and gazed down at her.

If the message on the wireless hadn't already done so, Michael's words and the anxious look in his gorgeous brown eyes would have cast away any doubts Anita had ever had about his feelings for her.

"I was worried about why you didn't mention loving me in your letters," she admitted. "But when I heard the message on the wireless . . ."

"I wrote in to the programme a few weeks ago when I wasn't sure I'd get here on time," he said. "I knew you and your folks always listen to it. That song of Bing's was the only way I could let you know how I feel."

"It was lovely," Anita said. "Really romantic."

Michael smiled as he quoted some of the words from the song.

"Tell me my fate. May I hear you say 'I do'?"

"Come to the gate and I'll answer you there," she whispered.

As they stood by the gate, entwined in love, Anita pointed to the snowdrops.

"Remember the day you went away, Michael? Just like our love, the snowdrops have kept blooming. There are more of them now, of course, and I'm not sure if I could love you any more than I do already. I love you with all my heart, Michael, and my answer is yes." ■

## Bunty 1960

THE Sixties were a time of great change for everyone. 1960 was a busy year for the Royal Family, who celebrated the birth of Prince Andrew and the wedding of Princess Margaret to Antony Armstrong Jones.

Four young men from Liverpool performed their first concert under the name of the Beatles in a Hamburg club, and a legend was born. In this Olympic year there were more celebrations in Rome when the British team came back with two gold, six silver and 12 bronze medals. Little girls had more reasons to be cheerful that year as "Bunty" released its first annual, two years after the popular comic had appeared.

There were familiar friends from the weekly comic. "The Four Marys", "The Dancing Life Of Moira Kent", "Lynn Raymond, Air Stewardess" and "Toots" all turned up. Then there were interesting picture features on "The Language Of Flowers", "Molly's First Riding Lesson", showing how to mount a pony properly and sit correctly in the saddle, and "The Story Of Coppelia". With a selection of longer reads and things to make and do, what more could a girl want? ■

41

# Tea At The Allotment

### by Bridget Aylott Nolan.

**M**ARION awoke as the first shaft of sunlight squeezed through her bedroom curtains. She felt as nervous as a schoolgirl reading aloud in class.

As she prepared her breakfast, she tried to concentrate on the milky tones of the radio presenter, but it failed to take away that worried excitement in her stomach.

Marion's eyes glazed in tender reminiscence as she looked out of the kitchen window and across the lawn to their bench. She and Fred would sit for many a happy hour sipping wine or tea, reading a book or doing a crossword together.

She laughed to herself now as she remembered Fred's frustration when she solved a clue before him.

"Don't tell me, don't tell me!" he'd cry. "I'll get it in a minute." And he always did, with the help of his trusty dictionary and his tired old thesaurus.

Hattie miaowed noisily as she rubbed herself around Marion's legs. Marion scooped the cat up into her arms and hugged her close to her chest.

"We do miss him, don't we, Hattie?"

Fred had died three years ago. They had known he was ill, but it had still come as a terrible blow to be parted from her husband of 35 years. Tears threatened to fall as Marion recalled his kind blue eyes, sparkling right to the end.

There had been no children to ease her grief, but she had friends and did not feel sorry for herself. She had enjoyed a wonderful life with Fred and had many special memories to make her smile. Her only regret, however, was that he didn't get the chance to develop his "retirement project" as he had always hoped.

"You've got to take it now that you've waited all this time," her friend, Tina, had said to Marion when she'd received the letter offering her an allotment.

"No. I mean to tell them I no longer want it, not with Fred gone," Marion told her. "It just wouldn't be the same. And besides, I'm not sure I could manage it on my own."

"But you're not a complete novice, Marion." Tina smiled. "You and Fred were always in the garden. You've been waiting, how long, six years?"

"Nearly seven."

"Well, there you go, then. Who knows how long you'll be waiting again if

you don't take this chance?"

"But it was Fred's idea . . . his project." Hot tears sprang to Marion's eyes.

"I know," her friend said, laying a hand on her arm. "I just don't want you to regret your decision. It could be just what you need right now, to meet people and have a new focus in life."

"But on my own, Tina? I just don't know."

"How much did you want an allotment when you went on the waiting list? Score out of ten!"

"Probably a seven," Marion mused.

"And how much do you want an allotment now?"

Marion sat back in the chair and folded her arms in quiet contemplation.

"Probably still a seven," she admitted, "but my confidence feels like a zero!"

"You either want an allotment or you don't." Tina laughed. "We can work on your confidence. And I want fresh-cut flowers all year round!"

✳    ✳    ✳    ✳

Marion smiled to herself now at her friend's encouragement. They had been as good as sisters for over 20 years. Marion sniffed and blinked hard at the thought of Tina's kindness and support in recent times.

Hattie miaowed as she rubbed her head under Marion's chin.

▶

"Oh, Hattie, this is ridiculous, look at me! You must think me a silly old girl. There you are, darling."

The cat purred as Marion set down a dish of food for her before getting herself ready.

She still felt afraid. She had not done anything of significance on her own for over 40 years, since before she met Fred at the college end-of-year dance. She knew Tina was right, that she needed to be brave, and this was a good first step towards a different life. She held her husband in her heart, always, but she still had her own life to live.

AND that was why, on this crisp autumn morning, Marion set off in her anorak and her wellington boots. It was a distance of only a mile or so to the allotment from her house. The trees on either side of the road were becoming bare, though this laid open a new beauty – splashes of silvery-green colour and a hoary array of barks. This, along with the crunch of the reds, yellows, browns and oranges of the leaves, made for a pleasant walk.

The gate opened with a click and Marion picked her way along a narrow grassed pathway to look for allotment number 17. It was early in the day and she couldn't see anyone around.

When she found her patch, it stood out for all the wrong reasons. Where the other areas had shrubs and trees, she had brambles and ivy. Where the others had vegetables and fruit, she had weeds and nettles. Clearly this allotment had lacked attention in recent years.

Marion felt her inexperience wash over her. She had not even thought to bring any tools with her, though she had remembered her new gardening gloves.

What had she been thinking of? She didn't know anything about plants!

"I don't know what to do with it!" she wailed out loud.

"Hello, there!"

Startled, Marion turned to see a man of about her own age smiling back at her. She felt embarrassed; surely he must have heard her. Ridiculously, she felt tears sting her eyes.

"Hello, there," the man repeated, "are you taking over old Alf's plot? You're brave. Mind you," he said encouragingly, "it isn't half as bad as it looks. It just needs tidying up. And the soil's beautiful. There's a lot of manure gone into that over the years. We've all been quite envious of the variety and quality of vegetables Alf managed to grow."

"Oh," Marion stammered, "well, I'm not much of a gardener, really. To be honest, I'm not sure if I've done the right thing now."

"It's the best thing in the world, and you'll be hooked in no time." The man laughed. "I'm Frank." He smiled as he offered a warm handshake.

Marion introduced herself and gladly shook hands. Her worries of the plot started to dissipate and she felt a little more confident as she smiled back at

Frank's friendly face.

"Fancy a cup of tea, Marion?"

They sat outside Frank's shed as the kettle boiled on the gas ring inside. They were soon joined by fellow allotment holders and Marion could see that this was the usual way to start the day here.

The kettle whistled and, as Frank prepared mugs of tea, Marion chatted to John and Diana, a couple who had kept their plot for more than twenty years. They used to grow fruit and vegetables as their family grew up, but now they enjoyed tending to their shrubs and flowers.

Then there was Janet, who had taken over her plot just a couple of years ago. She grew mostly potatoes and tomatoes.

"It's easy stuff to grow," she confessed to Marion.

Kerry turned up, then Dave and Karen, and Irene brought a packet of biscuits. Marion was welcomed as one of the group, a fellow gardener, and her reservations soon slipped away.

The tea was more delicious than any she had ever had. The taste, mingled with the warm sunshine, the woody, fruity air and the sound of the relaxed, welcoming chat of her new friends, made her happy to be here.

When they dispersed, Marion began to clear her allotment. She uncovered a rusty old burner and began to fill it.

"If you get any leaves, keep them separate," Frank called as he watched her. "You don't want to throw away leaves; they make lovely mulch."

Marion didn't know what mulch was, but she dutifully heaped up the leaves in a corner of her patch.

"Use these. I don't need them today," Frank offered as he came over with a wheelbarrow and a rake.

As Marion thanked him, her cheeks reddened and she felt like a shy schoolgirl. Nervous excitement skipped back into her stomach. As she pulled the rake through the weeds, she thought, or imagined, that Frank had held her gaze. It was certainly long enough for her to notice her own reflection in his chocolate brown eyes.

His eyebrows were still of an auburn hue and his thick hair was more white than grey. He was a very handsome man, Marion observed to herself. For a moment, convinced she had said that out loud, she grew redder and bowed her head and got on with her work.

L ATE in the afternoon, Marion arrived home exhausted and very happy. The exercise had been good for her and she was pleased to have met such a pleasant group of people.

"Hello, Hattie, my darling!"

Hattie jumped up on to Marion's lap as she sank into the settee for a rest with a cup of tea and a magazine.

"I'll feed you soon, my love – just let me have a breather. I've had a wonderful time! Everyone was so friendly, Hattie. Especially Frank."

Marion caught her breath. She wanted to laugh and she wanted to cry. She felt a sea of emotion roar inside her; of happiness and guilt, love, grief and fear of the unknown. The feelings rose in her throat until she felt overwhelmed.

At that point, the telephone rang.

"Oh, Tina, I'm so glad it's you!" Tears of relief ran down Marion's cheeks.

"Are you all right? Do you want me to come round?" her friend asked.

"No . . . no, you don't have to do that, really," Marion assured Tina as she took out a tissue to dry her eyes. "I've had a lovely day."

"Then what's upset you?" Tina asked with real concern.

"I just feel happy. I haven't felt that for a long time. And I'm not sure if I should be. Not yet, anyway . . ." Marion's voice trailed off.

"Marion, love, it's OK to feel happy." Tina, who had experienced the loss of her own husband some ten years previously, spoke with quiet certainty. "You were everything to Fred. You don't really think he would have expected you to deny yourself happiness for the rest of your life, do you? I know how hard it is, I really do. And I'm with you. Now, I want to know all about it."

Marion cheered up at her friend's curiosity and proceeded to tell her about her day at the allotment.

"They sound a great bunch of people," Tina said, "and that Frank was very kind to you."

"He was," Marion enthused. "I think I'd have turned around and come back home if he hadn't appeared when he did."

"Well, you enjoy yourself, chum. I'll be round next week with a couple of cakes and you can update me on your progress," Tina said before she hung up.

THE autumn days turned into winter weeks, but then, slowly, the signs of spring burst into life. Tightly wrapped leaves started to show on trees, tiny pink buds swelled on rose stems, and brave young snowdrops and crocuses started pushing through the hard earth.

Marion's confidence had grown with experience and with the encouragement of her gardening friends. She also enjoyed many conversations with Frank, and learned that he had lived alone since his wife died five years previously. Their only son had lived in Australia for many years, and Marion found she had a lot in common with Frank. They both enjoyed being near the sea, reading, doing crosswords, watching comedy and old movies.

Frank's favourite film was "Casablanca", and Marion loved the Alastair Sim version of "A Christmas Carol". Frank read Peter James, whilst Marion read Charles Dickens. Marion liked cats and Frank preferred dogs. They laughed a lot and Marion found it increasingly quiet when she got home each day.

She was contemplating inviting Frank over for a cup of tea for some time.

"It wouldn't be bad, would it . . ." she said to Hattie at the end of another satisfying day on the allotment ". . . to have a bit of company now and again? I'm sure he would love you, my darling."

Hattie purred approvingly. But that didn't soothe Marion's heart.

*   *   *   *

"Do you think it would give the wrong impression if I invited Frank over for tea?" she asked Tina as they shared lunch one afternoon.

"That depends what impression you want to give." Her friend grinned.

Marion laughed.

"Be serious! I just want to, well, would it be right?"

"Marion," Tina said emphatically, "you are a grown-up. If you want to invite Frank to tea, then do it. You've known him for some time now and that's what friends do, isn't it?"

The two women smiled at each other and chatted on into the afternoon.

MARION'S gardening tool kit had grown and she bought herself a small storage shed. Frank erected it for her in the corner of her allotment, opposite the compost bin that he had built for her using a couple of old doors and corrugated tin.

Her allotment had been transformed into a more ordered plot with a small vegetable patch and some raspberry canes. One corner was given over to flowers of all kinds, including daffodils, tulips, lily of the valley and dahlias. Dotted around the whole patch were roses, a favourite of Marion's.

She now knew the value of her heap of leaf mulch which she had covered in an old tarpaulin donated by Frank. She uncovered it one morning to see a creature slither past her feet. She squealed and Frank came over.

"What is it?"

"A snake! I just saw a snake!"

"How big was it?"

"About six inches long, and brownish-yellowish in colour."

"About the diameter of this finger?" Frank asked as he took her hand and pointed to her first digit.

"Yes," Marion answered sheepishly.

Frank roared with laughter.

"That's no snake, girl, that's a slow worm! He won't do you any harm."

He gave her a hug and kissed her on the forehead. He still had hold of her hand. Marion blinked as they both stood there like teenagers on a first date. She saw her reflection in his eyes again as he looked back at her.

"Frank, would you like to come round to my place some time for a cup of tea?" she blurted out.

Frank's smile broadened.

"I'd love to," he said, squeezing her hand.

"Well, now," he went on after clearing his throat, "you won't be afraid of slow worms any more."

He took up Marion's spade and showed her how to turn the mulch before loading it into her wheelbarrow.

"Just dig a bit in here and there to enrich the soil. Especially around the roses."

* * * *

The next day, Marion arrived at Tina's house with a big bunch of freshly cut daffodils and two large Viennese whirls from the bakery. She sat down in Tina's warm kitchen, her cheeks glowing and a real sense of happiness about her.

"You asked him, didn't you?" Tina smiled knowingly.

"Yes." Marion laughed. "And he said yes! And these are for you, my friend. Thank you for pushing me to do something with myself. I still miss my Fred every minute of the day, but I'm now living with his loss, instead of not living, if you know what I mean."

"I know exactly what you mean," Tina said reassuringly, "and it would make Fred very happy to know that. Now, I want to tell you all about my new pottery class. If you're going to be bringing me all these flowers, then I need a very classy vase in which to put them!"

Tina took out from a box a very sorry-looking attempt at a vessel, lopsided with an uneven base that made it rock. Marion and Tina rocked, too, with laughter.

ONE late April afternoon a frosty chill descended on the allotment site, but the growing spring sun still shone as Marion put a match to the burner. She stood back in delicious satisfaction, her cheeks glowing with warmth and exertion. She did not notice how sore her roughened hands were; she felt elated and alive.

Frank signalled to her that the kettle had boiled and she joined him at his shed.

"I've got a present for you," he said as she sat down next to him.

He handed her a bucket. In it was a rose bush. Marion looked at the label: *Ingrid Bergman.*

"A rose for a rose," Frank declared. "And, Marion, I'd like you to be my leading lady."

He took her hand and kissed it. She blinked back tears as Frank put his arm around her. They chatted, enjoying each other's company, as the wood smoke clung to them, the mud dried on their boots and the sun grew drowsy.

"Let's go to the seaside tomorrow," Frank suggested. "We could have fish and chips. There's a good garden nursery on the way. And on the drive down, you can give me some tips on growing raspberries. I've never had any luck with those." He smiled fondly.

Marion smiled back as they sipped their tea. It had never tasted so good. ■

48

*Illustration by Mandy Murray/Thinkstockphotos.*

# The White Lady

## — by Rebecca Holmes. —

I MUST admit I'm puzzled, and more than a little disappointed," Evelyn Johnson said. "I really thought Professor Parr would have been keen to help."

Mandy could understand her frustration. When the Friends of Winterfield Hall committee had heard that Professor Robert Parr was renting a cottage in the village for a few months, the news had seemed almost too good to be true.

With his name appearing regularly in all the history magazines, they'd been sure he was exactly the person to help publicise their cause. Evelyn, as secretary, had sent a diligently drafted letter, but had received no reply.

"Perhaps he's been too busy," George, their chairman, suggested. A retired teacher, he'd shown numerous parties of schoolchildren round the

49

old house, and also gave Mandy advice whenever she needed it.

"I read somewhere he's working on a book," he continued. "It might be better to let matters rest for a while."

Evelyn sighed.

"We don't have a while! You've seen the latest figures. We need to bring in more visitors and more money, or there won't be enough to carry out even the most urgent repairs."

"Maybe a couple of us could call round and introduce ourselves?" Mandy suggested. "A personal approach might work better."

"James is moving back from Canada this weekend, but I could spare an hour or two on Saturday," Evelyn said.

"I'll be free then, too," Mandy added.

"Fair enough," George agreed. "Just the two of you, mind. I don't think he'd take kindly to having a whole group turn up on his doorstep."

The warm stone building of Winterfield Hall, with its mullioned windows and dark timbers, had always captured Mandy's imagination. As a child, she'd devoured every tale she could about the house and its occupants. She knew all about Lady Catherine, the ghostly "White Lady" who was rumoured to wander the gardens, as well as the financial ruin of the family which had forced them to sell the house they'd loved and lived in for four centuries, after which it had fallen into total disrepair.

When, thanks to local support, the Hall had eventually been restored and opened to the public during Mandy's teenage years, she'd been one of the first through its doors. She'd returned to the area to teach at the local school, so helping as a volunteer at the Hall had been a dream come true.

Now, with extensive roof repairs needed, it looked as if everyone's work could be in vain.

ON Saturday, when Mandy called at Evelyn's house, she was surprised to see a man of about her own age, with short blond hair and gentle grey eyes, standing in the kitchen eating a bowl of cereal.

"Mandy, this is James, my son," Evelyn said.

He held out his hand in greeting.

"Hi." Although he smiled, he looked tired. "Sorry if I made my mum late."

"He just got in a few hours ago after a long flight, so he's still jet-lagged, I'm afraid," his mother explained. "The sooner we can get you rested and fed properly, the better! Right, let's go and charm our man. " She picked up her bag.

"I know James hates me fussing, but I can't help it," Evelyn confided as they walked along the pavement in the chilly spring wind. "He has been away for nearly three years, and he's had a dreadful time since his girlfriend broke off their relationship. At least he has some job interviews lined up here."

Soon they were pushing open the cottage's garden gate and walking up the crazy-paved path.

Mandy wasn't sure what to expect when the door was opened. An ageing academic in a tweed suit? Certainly not someone tall and slim wearing jeans and a checked shirt. He looked as though he'd be just as much at home striding among ancient ruins in far-flung places as in an old weaver's cottage tucked behind a parish church in northern England.

"Can I help you?"

She opened her mouth, but no words came out.

Evelyn took over.

"Good morning, Professor Parr. I'm Evelyn Johnson, and this is Mandy Carlton. We're volunteers at Winterfield Hall, that lovely old stately home down the road. I do hope we haven't called at a bad time?"

"Of course not," he replied. "I was just about to stop for coffee. Come in. And please call me Robert."

He showed them into a large sitting-room made blissfully warm by a log fire. At one end, a large table was almost buried under books and papers.

"I remember seeing something about the Hall a few days ago," he said once Evelyn had outlined the contents of the letter she'd sent. "Letters tend to get buried on my desk, but I'll do my best to help. It would be a shame if the Hall didn't get the help it needs, especially with such an enthusiastic team."

"And knowledgeable," Evelyn said. "Mandy's a history graduate, you know."

"Really?" He turned to her. "What do you do?"

Mandy felt herself blushing.

"I teach at the local school. History has always been a passion, though."

"Several of our volunteers will be in the King's Arms later," Evelyn said. "Everyone meets there. Do come. You'll be made very welcome."

Robert turned to Mandy again.

"Will you be there?"

"Probably. I pop in most Saturday nights."

"Good. As a fellow historian, you'll be able to tell me more about the Hall."

IN the King's Arms that night, Mandy found herself looking at the entrance door every time it opened. It always brought in a cold draught, but never Robert Parr. Still, she had a cosy seat near the fire.

James was there, too, with a group near the dartboard. He came across.

"Can I get you a drink?"

"I'm fine, but thanks anyway. How are you settling in?"

"Not too badly." He perched on a stool by her table. "It feels strange being back after all this time, almost as if I'm a child again."

"I know what you mean. I'm lucky to have a job and somewhere to stay."

"That's what I'm hoping for. My parents are great, but Mum does tend to treat me as if I were about twelve!"

Mandy glanced round as the door opened again. This time Robert Parr stepped in, looking round the room as he unwound his scarf.

He smiled and strode over.

"Sorry I'm late. I had to finish a chapter on the Normans, and they didn't want to let me go!"

After being introduced, James muttered something about being needed for a game of darts, and Mandy was left alone with Robert.

"So, tell me more about Winterfield Hall and how you got involved," Robert said when he came back with their drinks.

She told him about its history, and how local people had set up a trust fund to save it when it had been earmarked for demolition.

"It's gradually been restored. We do everything we can to keep it that way."

Goodness, but his eyes were a rich chocolate brown. And deep, and –

"That must take a lot of work."

She gathered her thoughts.

"It does, but it's worth it. And it's part of the community. Not only is it open most days, but there's also a restaurant which is very popular. Then there are the weddings, and even ghost hunts! Having someone like you at one of our events would provide welcome publicity and encourage even more visitors."

"I'm flattered, but I'm not exactly famous."

"You're well known. After all, you've had lots of articles published, and didn't I hear you being interviewed on the radio last month?"

AFTERWARDS, Robert walked Mandy home. The route took them past the entrance drive to the Hall. In the dark the building couldn't be seen, although she could sense its presence.

"People sometimes claim they see the White Lady, Lady Catherine, when they come past here at night," she remarked.

"She was quite the matriarch of the family for a long time, wasn't she?"

"That's right. Apparently, she lived to a ripe old age, and is said to wander the grounds, making sure everything's in order. Some visitors even claim they've glimpsed her at the back of the room at weddings, nodding in approval as couples take their vows."

"Have you ever seen her?"

"No, and I don't expect to," Mandy said. "I think some places hold a kind of imprint of those who have lived there, if you know what I mean. But I also think a lot of people have overactive imaginations!"

"Call round during the week with a list of planned events," Robert said when they reached her flat. "We can check how they tie in with my commitments."

It took Mandy longer than usual to get to sleep with so many happy thoughts racing through her head. Not least was the prospect of meeting Robert again.

It was, however, a shock when she arrived at his cottage a few days later to find him in the process of packing.

"I'm moving on, I'm afraid," he explained. "A chance has come up to front a television documentary about my old friends, the Normans. The original presenter had to pull out at the last minute, and someone put my name forward. It's a fantastic opportunity. Even better, it's being filmed in France." He smiled apologetically. "It looks as if I could be away for a while."

"I imagine that the weather will be better," she said, swallowing her disappointment. "Can I give you this list of events, anyway? You might be back in time for at least one of them."

"I'll try my best, but I can't make any promises."

Mandy walked away from the cottage feeling pleased for Robert, but she also couldn't help feeling let down.

A RE we all ready for tomorrow?" George asked. Everyone around the table in the King's Arms nodded, including Mandy and James. "Good. Well, the weather forecast looks promising. People will be glad of a decent day out, after the long winter we've had. As this is the largest event ever held at Winterfield Hall – in modern times, anyway – I suggest we all get an early night."

He glanced at his watch.

"Or, should I say, not too late a night?"

After the initial disappointment over Robert Parr, the committee had pulled together and got on with making plans. Everyone had worked hard preparing for the spring fair.

James had also joined in, and his enthusiasm was infectious.

Mandy enjoyed his company. They always found plenty to chat about, and soon discovered that they shared the same sense of humour.

After the meeting, he walked her home, as he had on several occasions. This might be one of the last times, though. He'd mentioned earlier that he'd been offered a job near London.

"I never thought I'd get so fond of a place or so interested in its history," he said as they passed the Hall, invisible in the darkness. "It's funny, really. I only got involved to take my mind off . . ."

He stopped abruptly.

"What was that?"

Mandy hadn't seen anything apart from the headlights of a car approaching along a side lane that joined the main road.

"I thought I saw something near the house. Something white," James explained.

"Surely you don't mean Lady Catherine?" Mandy asked, laughing.

"Wouldn't that be awesome?" James replied. "Let's investigate!"

They made their way up the driveway. At this late hour, the crackling of twigs underfoot and rustling of night-time creatures in the undergrowth seemed unsettling.

Mandy suddenly realised she was holding hands with James, as if in unspoken agreement to guide each other through the darkness.

But when they arrived at the Hall they found nothing untoward.

"Probably just a trick of the light," James said.

The going was easier on the way back, yet they still held hands. Mandy felt a deep sense of contentment which was swiftly replaced by sadness as she realised how much she would miss James when he moved away.

"I wish you weren't leaving," she said as they came nearer to the road and the lights of the village.

"I wish I wasn't, either, even though I'm relieved to have found a job," he replied.

"After Shelley and I split up, it felt as if there was this big black cloud permanently hovering over me. I can't believe how much everything's changed for the better."

The first drops of rain began to fall, gently pattering on newly opened leaves.

"I'll definitely be back as often as I can. At first I thought coming home might be a backward step, but I feel differently now, especially since –"

He stopped as a car pulled up a few feet ahead of them.

"Can I offer you young people a lift?" George asked as they drew level. "You're going to get a soaking."

Even as he spoke the words the rain seemed to get heavier.

"See what I mean about the cloud?" James chuckled as they climbed into the back.

Mandy was glad to take shelter, but that didn't change the fact that a moment had been lost. She couldn't help wondering what James had been about to say to her.

I F any former occupants of Winterfield Hall really did haunt their old home, they would have been more than a little surprised to see the goings-on of the next day, not to mention confused as to which century they were in! Visitors thronged both building and gardens, making the most of the spring sunshine. Volunteers wandered round in period costume.

James was dressed as a minstrel, complete with a battered old guitar that he kept strumming as he told everyone to imagine it was a lute. George clearly enjoyed cutting a dash as a cavalier.

Evelyn, as a Tudor Lady of the Manor, was leading guided tours under the gaze of old family portraits, while there were far too many "priests" to have a hope of all squeezing into the priest-hole.

Mandy had come as one of several witches, and was entertaining a group of enthusiastic children with some of the more blood-curdling aspects of the Hall's history. She'd just finished an account of how an unfortunate family member was alleged to have been slain by the sword after a heated altercation when she was aware of someone standing behind her.

She turned to see, not the aggrieved gentleman concerned, but Robert Parr, of all people.

"Well told!" he said. "There's nothing like a gory tale for getting children interested in history."

"It rarely fails, in my experience," she agreed, somehow keeping her voice calm. "When did you arrive back?"

"About half an hour ago. I'd have let you know I was coming, but I wasn't sure until the last minute," he explained. "I've been wandering around, taking in the atmosphere. You've done an excellent job. The house feels so welcoming and alive.

"Now, I believe I have an engagement to keep. Come and help me track down the local press. We'll get this place some well-earned publicity."

LATER, everyone tidied up after a long and successful day. After talking to a reporter, who had promised that the Hall would feature prominently in the next edition, Robert had returned to the cottage for some much-needed sleep, assuring everyone he'd come along to the King's Arms later.

Mandy had carried on with the rest of the fair. She and James were last to leave.

She couldn't help thinking about their unfinished conversation from the night before.

"Hey, come and look at this," James called from one of the windows. "I think I've found our apparition from last night."

She went over, intrigued, to see him holding out a white muslin curtain that would have draped from the ceiling all the way to the floor, if half of it wasn't hanging out of the window.

"This catch needs seeing to," he said. "It comes undone if you don't press it down hard enough. I found this window slightly open, with the curtain hanging out. It must have been like that last night."

She remembered the headlights from the car, which would have pointed directly towards the Hall. It all made sense.

James pulled the curtain inside and bowed to it.

"Pleased to meet you, Lady Catherine."

'Watch out. She might take that as an invitation."

Their laughter was interrupted by the bleeping of his phone.

"A Tudor minstrel with a mobile phone?" Mandy asked. "Whatever next? An electric lute?"

As he read the text message, James's grin was replaced with a thoughtful expression. The abrupt change in mood set Mandy's heart pounding. What was wrong today? First the shock at seeing Robert, and now this!

At least with Robert the feeling had soon settled. She'd had a crush on him, that was all. But James was moving on. That was probably what the message was about.

To her surprise, once he'd finished reading, he looked directly at her, his eyes searching.

"It's a call back from a local company who interviewed me a couple of weeks ago. They'd like to offer me a position."

"That's wonderful news!"

"Yes," he agreed as they locked the main door and set off across the gardens. "It means I don't have to move away. Or, at least, I hope it means that."

Mandy frowned at his muted reaction.

"Why? Is the other job better paid?"

"Yes, although the cost of living is higher in London, of course. But that's not what I'm thinking of. Mandy, I . . ."

He turned to face her.

"What I was going to say last night, before circumstances interrupted us, is that you're the reason I'm glad I came back. After what happened last year, I thought I'd never love again. Yet the more I got to know you, the more I realised that wasn't the case. I wasn't sure if you felt the same, though. Someone like you will surely have lots of admirers, men like Robert Parr. That was obvious, that first night at the King's Arms."

Mandy gasped as the realisation hit her. At the time, she'd assumed he was just moving across the room to rejoin his friends, but looking back now it was clear that his confidence must have been shattered after the previous year's events.

"If you don't feel the same," James continued, "I'll understand. We can still be friends. But if my feelings are returned, then wild horses won't be able to drag me away from here."

"James, I feel the same," she answered, slipping her hand into his. "In fact, I was dreading you leaving! I can't imagine life without you."

No further words were needed as he gathered her into his arms for a lingering kiss.

When they both pulled away, a few moments later, he looked back at the Hall.

"Is that Lady Catherine, do you think, nodding approvingly from the window?"

Mandy laughed.

"Of course it isn't! It's the curtain, as well you know, though at least this time it's safely inside."

Still, she reflected as they walked on, arm in arm, in some ways she wouldn't have been surprised. Like everyone who'd ever been there, she and James were part of its history now. Its living history.

And somehow she knew that Winterfield Hall would have plenty of stories to tell for a long time to come. ■

## Godshill, Isle of Wight

**GODSHILL** is the quintessential English village, and boasts some of the oldest architecture on the Isle of Wight. With its delightful mediaeval church, charming thatched-roofed cottages and a winding main street lined with traditional tearooms, Godshill is as picturesque as it is popular.

Legend has it that the village got its name when the building of a church was begun at the bottom of the hill, but large stones kept disappearing overnight and reappearing at the site of the present church at the top of the hill. After two consecutive nights, work was restarted, but after the third removal of the stones it was assumed that God wanted the church built on the hill and hence the name Godshill was formed.

This 15th-century church has unusual churchyard monuments and is among the top 10 most-visited churches in the UK. ■

# The Magic Saucer

## by Em Barnard.

I'D shrugged off my coat and had just made a cuppa when a scream and shattering of glass swirled me round and into the lounge. My granddaughter was standing beside my glass-topped coffee table, still in her pink anorak, tears coursing. Spotting me, her wails soared in a need for comfort. Taking in the shards of saucer surrounding the upset cup on the table, gift box and wrappings at her feet, I dashed over.

"Tania, are you hurt, darling?" I checked her hands. She shook her head through sobs. I backed up and sat on the sofa, drawing her on to my lap for a cuddle. I could have kicked myself for expecting a six-year-old to set her gift aside without another peep. And now her dream was shattered, too.

Earlier this morning, with the weather threatening a wind-hurling downpour, we'd gone into town to buy her mum a Mother's Day gift. The vibrancy of the spring bouquet on the gold-inscribed *To Mother* cup and saucer caught her eye. It was the last on the stand. She'd been so bright and bubbly, chattering about it all the way to my house.

An earth-juddering roll of thunder and suddenly the window-panes began to cry, too. Tania's wails rose again, and within my china cabinet the magic saucer I'd made Mum as a child slipped from its perch. I smiled wryly at the similarity. But it got me wondering – could that same magic work fifty years on?

"Come on." I slipped Tania from my knee. "Let's get you out of your coat and wipe your face, then I'll tell you a story about a magic saucer I made for my mum when I was about your age."

"Magic saucer?" Through hiccupping sobs her eyes flicked to mine in curiosity as I led her into the hall.

"My teacher asked us to bring an old saucer to class, said we were going to make a magic one from it," I began as she dried her tears. "Said as soon as our mums held it, the magic would happen. And, you know, when I gave mine to Mum, it did just that."

"What sort of magic?"

"Ah, well, you only find that out if you make one for your mum. It's easy to make. Come on, I'll show you the one I made. When Mum went to heaven the magic saucer came back to me."

She slipped from her chair and followed me. When I opened the china cabinet the saucer rolled out and stopped at my feet.

58

"See? It knows who made it." I reached for the *papier-mâché* saucer, gazing fondly at it. The pink mottled wallpaper was tan with age now, the rim fraying, showing the brittle frailty of the layers, the cut-out of pinks in its concave centre faded but still glued tight.

I handed it to Tania. She wrinkled her nose. I knew this was going to be a leap of faith for her.

I dropped to my haunches.

"Tania, how about you making a magic saucer like this for your mum? She's always loved mine."

It was true, Carol had often been intrigued by it. Plus, she already had a collection of Tania's scribblings, the forerunners to such hand-made gifts.

When I emptied Mum's china cabinet after her passing, the saucer was among a crush of greetings cards and novelties I'd made for her. But I'd forgotten what she'd written on the base of the saucer.

*Katy. Made at school. Age seven. 1955.*

When I found she'd dated every single gift I'd made her, I crumpled into a chair and wept.

TANIA was still twitching her nose.

"We can nip out tomorrow and buy some flowers, maybe find another cup and saucer," I encouraged. "But if I drop this one it won't break." I did so. "See? That's part of the magic. Let me put it away, it's precious to me."

When I looked at her she was staring at the shards, biting her lip. I knew she was considering.

"There's lots of gooey mess involved, a bit like baking. But if you don't want to get your fingers all sticky . . ."

At that, her eyes gleamed with interest.

I led her into the kitchen where I took a half dozen old saucers from a cupboard.

"Now, you have to choose, because the magic is coming through your fingers, not mine."

A finger hovered then swooped.

"That one, because it's got flowers on it."

"Perfect. Now we need newspaper. That's it," I said brightly, as sitting at the table she tore the sheet in concentration.

I switched the light on against the darkening sky, and the boiler to heat the radiators.

"Perfect," I praised her over the scattering of paper petals. "Now for the magic paste."

I set flour, water and a bowl on the table.

"I'll pour and you mix." Then I sang off the cuff, "Flour and water round we stir, until our hands become a blur!"

It splattered everywhere, but Tania's giggles were the ingredient that made the mix perfect.

"Hey, presto!" I whipped a new, one-inch paintbrush from its plastic casing. "Oh, it's covered in magic dust! You'd better have some." I tickled her round the face.

"Now, this is the sticky, tricky bit. You paste the petals on to the saucer, lots of petals and lots of paste. That's it. Both sides and over the rim, completely sealing the saucer. I'm just popping into the lounge to dig out my old birthday cards, so you can pick a picture for the centre."

I hurried off with unseen brush and pan to collect the shards. I placed the lonely cup in the china cabinet as a memory. I'd vacuum the lounge later once I'd put Tania to bed. She was staying overnight while my Carol was on morning shifts at the supermarket this weekend. Dad Tony had an early taxi call tomorrow morning to drive a fare the three-hour run to Heathrow Airport. We'd all meet at my house for a late Sunday lunch.

I was awake early, working on a brilliant idea for the saucer, when Tania peeped in.

"Is it dry yet?"

"Let's go and see."

In dressing-gowns, in the warming kitchen with radiator and light on against a chilly wet dawn, we stared at the two saucers – one paper, one china. Tania swung me a look of open-mouthed surprise.

"But how did the real saucer get out, Nana?"

"Well, like there are tooth fairies, there must be magic saucer fairies, too."

Aged ones in dressing-gowns and specs, I said inwardly. But it was the answer many of us in class had received when questioning our teacher. It was years later I realised she must have cut round all those rims, slipped out the real saucer, then pasted the two sections. All part of the magic. And she had had a week to do them.

Tania gave a gasp and shot me a delighted look.

"Come on, back to bed, it's early yet."

By nine she was standing over it again.

"Can I paint it now?"

She painted it the way I told her from my early dawn idea. And between that and lunch we popped to the supermarket.

From the kitchen I could hear Tania squeal in excitement at the arrival of her parents. I heard her run into the hall as I covered the roast chicken on the drainer to rest. Carol had a key, and by the time I entered the hall she greeted me as Tania tugged her into the lounge by her free hand, the other grasping the bunch of daffodils she had bought earlier.

I'd hoped to whisper a word about the saucer, but as I went to follow Tony barred my way with a huge bunch of sunny mixed flowers and a kiss. I thanked him, my mind and ears on Tania's giggles as she urged her mum to open her gift.

Holding Tania's magic saucer in both hands, the china cup sitting proudly on it, Carol looked bemused. My brilliant idea had been that Tania should paint it white and stick cut-outs of the same spring flowers adoring the cup round her saucer. Blue hyacinths. Red tulips. Yellow daffodils.

"It's a magic saucer, Mummy," Tania said. Then into her chest she mumbled, "The proper one got broken."

Tony squeezed my shoulder. He'd cottoned on. Then Carol's head lifted and she met my eyes fleetingly.

"You made me a magic saucer, Tania?" Her tone was a mix of delight and disbelief.

She set the cup aside and examined the saucer.

"Oh, Tanny, it's beautiful. My favourite spring flowers, too! It's the best and most precious gift you could ever have given me. I shall treasure it always." ▨

# Judy 1962

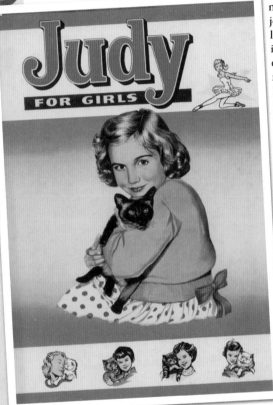

**THE** first "Judy" annual in 1962 marked a memorable year. The journey to school became a little safer after the introduction of Panda crossings, though these were replaced a few years later by Pelican crossings after both pedestrians and drivers found the Panda's flashing lights confusing! The flashing lights might have been welcome during that year's heavy smogs. Though not as bad as the great smog of 1952, conditions were so severe that 750 Londoners lost their lives.

There was brighter news in the world of entertainment. The instrumental "Telstar" by the Tornadoes commemorated the launch of the Telstar communications satellite, which made possible the first live transatlantic television signals. Teenagers' musical lives were never the same after the debut performance of the Rolling Stones at London's Marquee Club, while younger girls thrilled to the first Royal Ballet duet by Margot Fonteyn and Rudolf Nureyev.

Ballet was a popular topic in "Judy", with features and stories about the great ballets, ballerinas and life at ballet school. The first annual also included features on ice-skating and "Girls Who Sparkle In Sport", highlighting achievements across sports from archery, cycling, tennis, swimming, sailing and others – a great attraction for future hobbies, or even careers, for its young readers.

Other pages included pets, fashion and poems and puzzles, and, of course, stories from the weekly like the ever-popular "Colleen And The Last Witch" – the tale of Colleen O'Day, immune from magic as the seventh daughter of a seventh daughter, and her funny battles with Bumble, the last witch in Ireland. ■

*Illustration by Martin Baines.*

# Run, Rabbit, Run

---
### *by Samantha Tonge.*
---

**G**INA caught Rob's eye across the office and smiled, hoping that he hadn't noticed her mouth was full of shortbread. With his smart suits and wavy hair, he had made quite an impact since joining the company a couple of months ago.

As stylish secretary Megan laughed at one of his jokes, Gina scolded herself for judging Rob by his appearance – something she heartily disapproved of. With her love of food and generous figure, people who judged her that way were always surprised that Gina's other passion was swimming.

Rob's appearance wasn't his only attractive asset – he was clever and thoughtful, being the only one in the office who remembered she drank

63

decaffeinated coffee. Plus, he ran a youth club in town and told madcap tales of the teenagers' antics.

Gina stared at her computer and asked herself the question that had often popped into her head over recent weeks. Would a man like Rob ever be interested in a biscuit-addicted woman whose hair smelled of chlorine?

"Gina?"

She almost knocked over her pen pot as he sat down by her desk.

"Hi, Rob," she said, offering him a slice of shortbread.

Sometimes he came over for a chat and, despite his striking looks, Gina found him easy to talk to. He seemed to enjoy her company – but only as a friend, she'd tell herself.

"How was your camping weekend?" she asked. "Did all the kids behave?"

He took a slice.

"The two days were jam-packed with hikes, barbecues and treasure hunts. Luckily, the weekend passed without a single drop of rain." He bit into the biscuit. "Hmm, delicious. Home-made?"

Gina nodded.

"How about I get you a coffee to go with them?" he offered. "After I've, um . . ." Rob cleared his throat ". . . asked you a small favour."

"That sounds ominous!" Gina laughed.

"Not really." Rob smiled. "You like rabbits, right?"

"You know I do, after that conversation we had about pets last week." She grinned. "Anyway, yes, rabbits are great."

"So you'd be in favour of helping to raise money for that rabbit rescue centre on the outskirts of town?"

She nodded.

"Definitely."

"A few weeks ago the youth club visited it. At this time of year they're desperate for funding. Lots of people buy their kid a bunny for Christmas, but a few months later get rid of it as the novelty has worn off."

Gina tutted.

"Usually the rabbits get dumped outside the rescue centre in a box. We saw one in a right state, its fur all dirty and matted. It obviously hadn't been let out of its hutch for weeks."

"I bet the centre needs all the donations it can get," Gina said sensibly.

Rob swallowed his last bite of shortbread.

"Exactly. We've decided to run a sponsored race on Easter weekend – what with the Easter Bunny, we thought it was appropriate."

"What sort of race?"

"In Primrose Park, we'll set up a square-shaped course with four corners as rest stops, then divide participants into two groups. Half will wear bunny ears and get sponsored for how many sides of the square they can complete without . . ." he cleared his throat again ". . . without being caught by the

64

other group who are chasing them, dressed as dogs! Of course, the rabbits will have a ten-second head start. The dogs will be sponsored for how many they can catch."

Gina burst out laughing.

"So, how can I help? Handing out water? Making bunny ears?"

"How about running?"

"Me? Run?" Her cheeks burned red. Talk about being out of her comfort zone!

Swimming was a different matter, as Gina was confident after all her years of practice. But moving upright, one foot in front of the other, with all that perspiration and breathlessness? It was hard enough to look graceful in the water!

"Sorry, Rob. No way!" Gina shook her head.

"Why not? I've seen you at the pool, building up quite a pace," he said. "You're easy to spot, with that auburn hair flowing behind you."

Gina ran a hand through her waves, vowing to wear a swimming cap next time.

He wagged a finger.

"Don't even think of pretending that you aren't fit enough to take part."

"I haven't sprinted since I was at primary school," she stuttered. "Um, have you asked anyone else, like, say, Megan?"

"Yep, she's up for it. So is about half the office. Oh, go on, Gina – it'll be fun!"

Oh, dear. One of his lopsided grins meant that she said yes.

"Why, oh, why did I agree?" she asked her flatmate, Laura, as she strolled into their kitchen later that evening. Gina had just got back from her daily swim. "I'll look a right sight."

Laura stopped chopping for a moment and passed her a slice of carrot.

"If you ask me, he quite likes the way you look! Now, just relax – we've got two weeks. I'll help you train." Laura passed Gina another carrot stick and stared at her for a moment. "You'll be fine. And it's a way of getting to know this Rob better, isn't it?"

"I don't know what you mean!" Gina laughed, eyes twinkling.

GINA! Over here!" Rob called. About 30 teenagers milled around, wearing floppy felt ears and tails made from tights. She picked up her bag and made her way over to the huge oak tree. Easter Monday had come around far too quickly, she decided. At least the spring sunshine had finally shown its face after a weekend of torrential rain.

"Just in time," he said. "I was getting worried! I haven't seen you swimming this last week," Rob went on as he ticked off her name.

"No, my flatmate has been helping me train for this."

He glanced up.

"I'm impressed!"

"Bet I catch all you old fogies, anyway," a lad interrupted, whiskers drawn across his face.

"Fogies?" Rob replied. "Watch what you say, young Ben!"

"Yes, I'm like that bunny on the adverts," Gina put in. "All super-powered, thanks to the pile of Easter eggs I've eaten this weekend!" She bared her teeth. Ben laughed and ran off.

Rob stared at her.

"What? Have I got chocolate around my mouth?" she asked, blushing. "Must be from those mini eggs I ate on the way here. There's nothing like a bit of the brown stuff for settling nerves."

He gave his lopsided grin.

"No, it's just that you're clearly a natural with teens."

"My younger sister's taking her GCSEs this year. I like to think we get on well." Gina smiled. "Apart from when she stays overnight and goes home leaving my flat looking as if every cupboard and drawer has exploded and scattered its contents."

"Tell me about it. The youth club takes an age to tidy up on a Friday night. Although they're a good bunch of kids and often stay to help." He consulted his list. "Time to get cracking. Good luck, Gina." Rob bent over and picked up a pair of pink cardboard bunny ears which he gave her.

Stomach twisting a little, Gina put on the ears and stood next to Megan. Her smart colleague looked very professional, warming up with stretches.

Behind them, the posse of teenagers clapped and cheered, shouting out cheeky comments. Her mouth felt dry. What if she tripped over, or was caught straight away? Neither Rob nor Megan would think much of that.

GINA'S heart thumped as the threat of the chase pumped adrenaline around her body. The gun went off and she put down her head, legs moving faster than they had for years.

The teenagers stayed put and counted to 10. Slowly, Gina built up speed and squealed as she heard the whooping youngsters start to run. Must concentrate on my breathing, she told herself, trying to remember Laura's training tips.

Within minutes, screams came from behind as dogs tapped various bunnies on the back. Determined not to turn around and lose pace, Gina pushed forward, breathing evenly, as mud splashed up her clothes and squelched into her shoes.

She almost slipped, but regained her balance and finally reached the first rest stop. Now her chest heaved in and out and a trickle of perspiration ran down her face.

Rob was already there, bent over double to recover. He stood up and gave Gina the thumbs-up as more "rabbits" reached the bench.

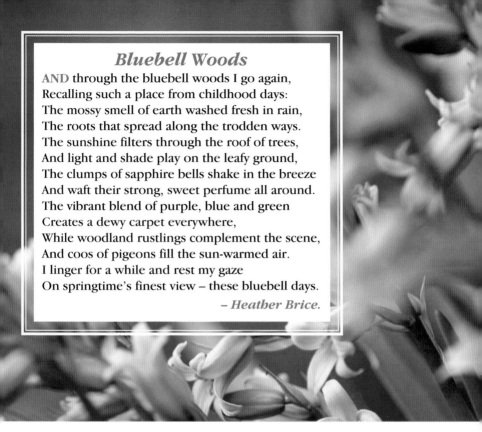

## Bluebell Woods

AND through the bluebell woods I go again,
Recalling such a place from childhood days:
The mossy smell of earth washed fresh in rain,
The roots that spread along the trodden ways.
The sunshine filters through the roof of trees,
And light and shade play on the leafy ground,
The clumps of sapphire bells shake in the breeze
And waft their strong, sweet perfume all around.
The vibrant blend of purple, blue and green
Creates a dewy carpet everywhere,
While woodland rustlings complement the scene,
And coos of pigeons fill the sun-warmed air.
I linger for a while and rest my gaze
On springtime's finest view – these bluebell days.

*– Heather Brice.*

"Well done," he said. "It looks like about eighty per cent of us made it to the first post." He puffed. "Megan got caught. She made the mistake of stopping to avoid a stretch of muddy turf."

Gina looked down at her legs and laughed.

"Perhaps I should have done that. I'll soon look like a chocolate bunny if I carry on like this!"

"I can just imagine you, head to toe in gold foil," Rob said, eyes twinkling. Was he flirting with her? Gina's stomach fluttered.

Before she knew it, the gun went off and she had to sprint to the second post, and then the one after that.

Almost an hour later, only five bunnies remained standing. Legs aching as if she'd swum a hundred lengths, Gina knew this would be her last sprint. Rob was purple in the face and smiled over at her just seconds before the gun went off.

Members of the public had stopped to watch and Gina yelped as one of them shouted at her to be careful, but it was too late. She felt tapping on her shoulder and turned to face young Ben.

"Well done," she said as they ground to a halt. "Looks like you caught me, after all."

He grinned.

"Guess you didn't run too badly . . . for an old fogey. Even Rob's been caught." Ben pointed ahead. In fact, all of the bunnies had failed to reach the rest stop.

Not long later, Rob joined Gina on the park bench. He carried a basket full of Easter eggs. Megan had refused one before leaving for home, muttering how the mud had ruined her designer socks.

HELP yourself," Rob told her, passing Gina the basket. "You deserve it. All that swimming has clearly given you amazing stamina."

"Don't mind if I do!" She picked out a large egg, took off its foil and bit into the top.

"Yummy," she said, eyes closed. They snapped open to find Rob gazing at her. Oops, that probably hadn't looked very delicate.

"Just refuelling the engine." Gina gave a nervous giggle.

"Don't stop on my account. It's nice to see a woman enjoy her food," Rob said. "My last girlfriend preferred a celery stick to chocolate and would rather eat those pre-packaged, calorie-counted meals than my home-cooked food."

He took an egg.

"It's not much fun eating out with someone who never orders anything but salad."

"Not much chance of that with me." Gina grinned before taking another bite. Rob's cheeks flushed.

"Good. Because I've been trying to find the right moment to ask you something. Do you fancy going out for a curry?"

Gina's heart almost stopped. Her eyes tingled as he took her hand.

"That sounds great!" she mumbled, wondering if he could hear her heart beat.

"Oh, Rob's going on a date with his very own bunny girl!" Ben called, suddenly appearing from behind them to grab the basket.

With mock anger, Rob shook his fist as the teenager laughed and ran off to continue handing out the eggs.

"Seems like you've got your hands full, looking after this bunch," Gina commented, heart still racing as she looked around at the teenagers. "Why don't we have that curry after this Friday's meeting? I could come and help out."

"Really?" Rob's eyes were shiny. "That's brill! I mean . . ." He leaned over and kissed her tenderly on the cheek.

Ignoring another teasing shout from Ben, the couple's fingers intertwined once more as they chatted about their favourite Indian foods. In fact, warmth surged across Gina's chest as if she'd just eaten a spicy meal. Stepping out of her comfort zone had really paid off, bringing her close to someone who made her feel very comfortable indeed. ■

Illustration by Stephanie Axtell.

# The Krispy Krunch Holiday

## by Annie Harris.

I ALMOST missed the final photographs. I'd piled the rest in an untidy heap, ready for us to sort through. Then, as I went to close the bureau drawer where Mum has always kept them, I heard a faint crinkle. Slipping my hand inside, my fingers closed on an envelope half-wedged into the back of the drawer.

I eased it out, then extracted one of the photos – and gasped.

Behind me, the door opened.

"Nearly finished, Becky?"

"What? Oh, yes, Alan." My mind was still far away. "These are the

69

last, I think."

My brother came across.

"Good grief!" He picked up the photo. "Brings it all back, doesn't it? Must be all of twenty-five years ago it was taken."

"Twenty-six. Got to be."

"Of course." He pulled up a chair and sat beside me. "Funny how it's all coming back. I remember it was freezing when we left Heathrow. Look, we're all in heavy jackets."

"Yes. It was like another world, wasn't it, arriving in the south of France? I couldn't believe how blue the sky was.

"Oh, look!" I pointed. "Surely – yes, there's that jam doughnut Paul insisted on shoving down him."

"Mum called him 'Hollow Legs'." Alan grinned. "He regretted that doughnut when we hit turbulence over the Alps!"

I groaned.

"We all regretted that doughnut – especially Mum when he missed the sick bag and got her skirt instead! I wonder if he's ever eaten one since?"

"We'll ask him. I'll pull his leg about it – greedy pig!"

We both smiled fondly down at the image of our brother. Alan was just a year behind me, Paul two years younger than him. He was dark and blue-eyed – like our dad, Mum always said, although we'd lost him before any of us could have any real memories of him.

Alan and I had the auburn hair of Mum's family – mine still was, with a bit of discreet help, while Alan's was greying now. Both of them, though, towered over me these days.

"Still," Alan mused, "if it hadn't been for him . . . What on earth was that revolting cereal called, anyway?"

"Let me think. Krunchy Krisps – no, Krispy Krunch, that was it."

"And what was that awful slogan? The one people had to complete?"

I screwed up my eyes, straining back through the years.

"For breakfast, tea or lunch, I love my Krispy Krunch because . . . because . . ." I laughed. "I've totally forgotten the punchline Paul wrote."

"With a bit of help from Mum, I suspect." Alan grinned.

"Whatever, he won!"

"Perhaps Paul won't even remember."

"Remember what?" Paul had appeared in the doorway. "Hi, sis."

He dropped a smacking kiss on my cheek and ruffled my hair.

"Hi, Al." He hugged his brother. "Remember what?" he repeated.

"Your Krispy Krunch slogan." I held out the photo to him.

"Good heavens! No, I don't. Still, I won, and that's all that matters. And it was a great holiday!"

"It was." I nodded. "Our first real holiday, with money always being so tight. And the first time abroad for any of us."

We were all so excited when the letter came to say that Paul had won first prize of a week's holiday in a seaside hotel in the south of France. We'd been over the moon, and we'd hardly been able to believe that we would also have our own photographer for the week.

MARK was waiting for us at Heathrow, complete with a very expensive-looking camera. He explained that he was freelance and had been going out to France anyway, as he was doing the illustrations for a new guidebook, so Krispy Krunch had hired him to do some shots of us for their next advertising campaign.

Except that the cereal bit the dust so fast that there never *was* another campaign.

"Do you remember," I said now, shuffling through the photos, "how we all had to be snapped eating Krispy Krunch and looking as if we loved it? Here, this one." I picked up another picture.

"That's the one!" Alan laughed. "You and me toying with our spoonfuls, trying not to look queasy, and Paul shovelling the ghastly stuff down like there was no tomorrow!"

"I really liked it!" he said defiantly.

"You would!" Alan and I chorused, then I went on.

"We had to have it every morning – I remember hating all the other guests who were stuffing themselves with croissants and *pain au chocolat*!"

"But the other meals were great," Alan admitted. "Remember that *boeuf bourgignon* we had for Sunday lunch?" He rolled his eyes at the memory. "You know, I believe my love of French cooking started there and then!"

'I'm sorry Mireille can't make it," I said.

"I know." He grimaced. "She was coming, of course, and bringing Emilie and Maxime. We were leaving Jean-Claude, our brilliant *maître d'*, in charge for the weekend, but he's gone down with that summer-flu-type bug, so she's had to stay – we've got a big wedding reception tomorrow. But we're going to close down for a week once the season's over, and we'll all come then."

"How about you, Becky?" Paul asked. "Is Rob going to be here?"

"I'm hoping so. He should be doing Heathrow to Singapore tomorrow, but he's trying to change his shift."

It was Paul's turn to riffle through the photos. He held one up for me to see and we all laughed. There was the thirteen-year-old me, looking a bit overwhelmed. The pilot and co-pilot smiled at me while I stared mesmerised at the control panel with its mass of illuminated dials.

"How soon did you decide?" Alan asked.

"Oh, before I even got back to my seat, I should think."

"People still do a double-take when I tell them my sister's an airline pilot," Paul remarked.

"I know, even though there are lots more of us nowadays." I hesitated, then went on. "But anyway, I'll be grounded for a while. I – we've – just found out that I'm pregnant."

"Oh, wonderful! At last! Congrats, sis!" They both hugged me and I felt tears prickle my eyes.

Y OU know, I've never really considered it before, but this . . ." I tapped the pile of photos ". . . it shaped all our lives, didn't it? Not that we knew it at the time, of course."

"You're right," Paul agreed. "It certainly did for me. Mark was great – he let me trail after him with my little Kodak, getting in his way when he was trying to take shots for that book. And when we had that day up in the gorge."

"Verdon?"

"Yes!" He picked out another picture, of Alan and me in a canoe with towering cliffs behind us. "He spent ages explaining to me how he'd lined up the back lighting and had got just the right angle for this one shot."

"We thought it was going to be just a fad," I confessed.

"But it wasn't, was it?" Alan said. "Saw your wildlife pics, bruv, in 'National Geographic' a couple of weeks back. They were great! Young Emilie was very impressed with her uncle Paul – wants a camera for her birthday!"

Paul was still sorting through the pack.

"There should be another one somewhere. Yes, here it is."

"Of course!" I exclaimed. "The one you took at that fête we went to, on the last evening."

He nodded.

"All week I'd been longing to get my hands on Mark's Leica, and finally he let me take just this one shot."

I was studying the picture, with the two figures in the foreground dancing together.

"Gosh, it's all there, isn't it? We couldn't see it at the time, of course, but you just have to look at their faces . . ."

The lounge door opened and our mother and stepdad came in.

"So you've found all those old photos!" Mum smiled up at Mark. "Goodness me, it seems like yesterday, doesn't it, love?"

"It certainly does. I'll never forget that evening, when we danced." Mark took up the very first photo, the one at the airport. "That reminds me. On the sofa – squeeze up, all of you. In the right order, now!"

We obediently shuffled along – me, mum, Paul and Alan – and beamed at the camera.

"Oh, nearly forgot." Mark dug into his pocket, and produced a brown paper bag. He handed it to Paul, who pulled out . . . one jammy doughnut!

"Mind Mum's skirt!" I shook my finger. "Use the paper bag this time!"

We all collapsed with laughter just as the camera clicked. And the Silver Wedding celebrations had begun. ■

72

## *Torquay, Devon*

**THE ENGLISH RIVIERA** is a resort in the truest sense of the word, attracting visitors of all ages and interests throughout the year. Undergoing a waterfront regeneration and with a number of new attractions, Torquay has something for everyone and for all ages, at all times of the year.

Torquay has been one of the UK's top holiday destinations since Victorian times when the gentry promenaded, bathing huts were wheeled down to the beaches and anyone who was anyone had an attractive villa overlooking the sea.

It was the Victorians who first used the term "English Riviera" to describe their favourite resort and their legacy remains to this day, with sparkling white villas perched on the verdant hilltops, beautiful gardens around the seafront and elegant Victorian façades along the main streets. ▧

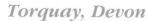

# Two By Two

## by Mary Kettlewell.

**F**AYE STANBROOK stood by the buddleia admiring the butterflies. Red Admirals flitted from flower to flower; Tortoiseshells, Painted Ladies and bright yellow Brimstones vied for the fragrant blossoms. Their beauty was matched by hers. Her long fair hair glistened in the sunshine. High cheekbones and striking green eyes were set off by the long floral dress she wore and the straw hat adorned with a posy of primroses.

What a contrast to the tall young man who tore wild-eyed into the churchyard! Mr Daubeny, the architect overseeing work in St Mary's ad Vincula, her father's ancient church, could hardly splutter out the words.

"I must see the rector immediately."

She stared at his dust-covered face and shoulder-length hair, and waistcoat that was spotted with pieces of plaster.

"Mr Daubeny, whatever is the matter? You look as if the church steeple has toppled over."

"It's incredible, amazing! I can't believe it, Miss Stanbrook. The workman was using his chisel and a great area of plaster fell off. You've never seen anything like it."

Had he had a brainstorm, Faye wondered. She decided to let her father solve the mystery.

"The rector is in his study writing a sermon. I will tell him you are here."

Moments later the Reverend Silas Stanbrook appeared on the rectory steps smoking a meerschaum pipe, a quill pen between his fingers.

"Mr Stanbrook, sir. I have discovered Noah's Ark, together with a horde of strange animals."

Silas put on his stern look.

"Young man, have you been at the bottle?"

The architect, beside himself with excitement, caught hold of the rector's arm and tugged him in the direction of the church.

"No, Mr Stanbrook, but a miracle has occurred, no less. Come and see for yourself."

Father and daughter, thoroughly perplexed, followed him into the quiet interior of St Mary's ad Vincula. Scaffolding stood in a corner of the transept and a ladder snaked up to a high section of the wall. John Roach, the stonemason, stood on a narrow stretch of planking with hammer and chisel in hand. A great swathe of plaster had fallen away, exposing the delicate colours and lines of a once-hidden mediaeval wall painting of Noah's Ark.

74

Illustration by Mark Viney.

The rector gasped.

"It is an incredible find. A fresco hidden all these hundreds of years, only seeing the light of day this morning!"

The architect had regained his composure.

"I believe there may be other hidden paintings lying behind that old plaster."

Faye had pushed her way to the foot of the ladder and was staring up eagerly.

"I'm climbing up to have a closer look."

The rector put a hand on her arm.

"You shall do no such thing, child. It is far too dangerous."

"Don't fuss, Father. If it is safe for the stonemason, it is safe for me."

Before he could reply she was clambering up the steep ladder, skirts swirling, the architect following close behind should a helping hand be needed.

The rector sighed. Ever since losing his dear wife four years ago he had despaired of trying to bring up Faye as a genteel daughter of the rectory. Her outgoing nature, love of laughter and reckless daring had completely defeated him. At nineteen she was just as strong minded as her mother had been.

"Father, you must come up! There is a zebra, a giraffe, a lion, several peacocks, a snake and a dog about to enter the Ark!" Her warm laughter filled the aisle. "And look at old Noah. He's got a beard two feet long and a face like a dried apricot!"

The rector shook his head.

"I can see perfectly well from here, my dear," he said, peering through his pince-nez. He had no intention of ascending the ladder in his billowing cassock. He intended to preserve a hint of dignity, even if his daughter did not. What concerned him more than her lack of propriety was the enthusiasm with which the architect seemed to be showing his daughter the Ark.

"Can you see that bear in the distance, Miss Stanbrook? And there are Shem, Ham and Japheth, Noah's sons, looking nervously at the flood."

She moved closer and peered over his shoulder.

"What do you think that is, Mr Daubeny?" she asked, pointing to a blurred creature in pale yellow.

"I do believe it's a wild boar. Can you see the tusks on its snout? I trust that Mrs Noah keeps well clear of it!"

The rector listened to their cheerful conversation with growing unease.

"How did you first become involved with church architecture, Mr Daubeny?"

"By following the family tradition. Mother and Father are artists at the St Ives colony in Cornwall. I was fortunate enough to be offered a place at the Slade School of Art two years after its foundation in eighteen-seventy-one."

"And you specialised in church art."

"Yes, mainly paintings of an ecclesiastical nature."

"You must tell me more, Mr Daubeny. It is all absolutely fascinating!"

The rector cleared his throat and intervened.

"It is time we returned, Faye. Mrs Norris will chide us if we are late for luncheon."

Reluctantly she climbed down the ladder, helped by a most attentive Mr Daubeny.

\* \* \* \*

The rector scarcely tasted his roast beef and horseradish sauce. He was experiencing disturbing visions of artists. Were they not renowned for scandal and amoral behaviour?

After lunch and a fortifying glass of Madeira he joined his daughter in the drawing-room.

"Have you seen Richard Cornwell this week, Faye? I believe he is

76

busy with lambing."

"All he talks about is pigs, geese, sheep and cattle. That and his wealth."

"He is a good, solid, reliable farmer, my dear. I have long hoped that you will one day become his wife. He comes from a landed family and will be able to provide for you handsomely."

"He is as dull as ditch water, Father! I have no intention whatsoever of marrying so dour a fellow." Then came the words which sent her father's heart plummeting. "Mr Daubeny is far more amusing and entertaining."

"Daubeny is a young man in his twenties, scarcely established in the architect's world. As for his family, artists are notoriously fickle."

"I don't care for any of that. All I know is that Mr Daubeny is full of life and laughter, whereas Mr Cornwell is as dry as wheat chaff!"

Her father returned to his study, wishing his wife was at his side to share his concerns. Perhaps, if he let the matter drop, Faye would lose interest in the young man with the unkempt hair and dusty appearance . . .

THE following Saturday was the occasion of the May Fair in the rectory paddock.

"Will you be attending this year, Faye?"

"Indeed I shall, Father. I am to help Mrs Fanthorpe with her embroidery stall."

The day dawned, and for some time Faye aided Mrs Fanthorpe with her quilts and antimacassars. Then Mr Richard Cornwell, sombre in plus fours and a tweed cap, greeted her and began an interminable conversation centring around breeds of Highland sheep. She muttered an excuse before he could invite her out and made her way towards the tea hut, only to find herself face to face with Jonathan Daubeny.

His face brightened.

"Miss Stanbrook, I'm so pleased to see you! I was hoping that you would show me the delights of the fair, but I fear that your father does not approve of artists. He thinks we are unprincipled and feckless."

"Take no notice of Father, Mr Daubeny. He means no unkindness, and has what he considers to be my wellbeing at heart." She smiled and touched his forearm. "Now, let me take you to the conjuror's tent."

The rector, who was sitting outside enjoying a fairy cake and a glass of primrose wine, frowned as he saw Jonathan Daubeny take his daughter's arm and lead her across to one of the booths.

As he sipped his drink, the Reverend Silas Stanbrook determined to have a serious talk with his daughter as soon as was convenient.

\* \* \* \*

"Faye, I am not happy about your relationship with Mr Daubeny. You were in his company all the afternoon. It is hardly fair on Mr Cornwell."

Faye's eyes blazed.

"Father, I have not the slightest interest in Mr Cornwell. He is a dullard and talks continually of money."

"Your dear mother would have wished you to marry him."

"Nonsense, Father. I remember Mother saying to me that a woman should follow the dictates of her heart, not the expectations of society." She stared angrily at him. "Mr Daubeny has offered to accompany me to the parish rogationtide picnic. I can't believe it's forty days since Easter already! Anyway, I have accepted his offer."

The rector's usually benign face darkened.

"Then you are going directly against my wishes! A man from an artistic family is not a suitable suitor for a daughter of a man of the cloth."

He strode off to the rectory, leaving a heavy atmosphere behind. It was the first time he had ever fallen out with his beloved daughter and it pained him.

As for Faye, she, too, was distressed. She could tell that her father was hurt, yet she felt strongly that it was her right to decide with whom she wished to associate.

LATER that day the rector harnessed his new mare and fastened her between the shafts of the trap, ready to set out on his afternoon of parish visiting. She was frisky, and snorted indignantly as the reins were tugged.

Then one of the gamekeepers from the nearby wood fired a sally of shots at a flock of pheasants. The deafening reports caused the mare to rear and thunder forward at breakneck speed. The rector tussled vainly as the trap swayed. He expected at any moment to be thrown out on to the gravel drive. Faye looked on with horror, helpless.

A figure sprang out from the bushes surrounding the churchyard, a young man with long hair, covered in dust, wearing a red waistcoat. Jonathan jumped in close to the rearing animal, recklessly ignoring the flying hooves and snorting mouth. He grabbed the reins, put up an almighty fight and finally got the mare under control.

Together with Faye, who had run across, he helped the shaken rector to dismount and led him into the study, where they settled him into an armchair.

"Father, I'll fetch you a glass of brandy. You've had a dreadful shock."

But it was to Jonathan that he turned.

"Mr Daubeny, I cannot thank you enough for your brave action. Had you not mastered the mare I fear I would have ended up on the ground with who knows what injuries!"

"Thank goodness I witnessed the incident and was able to do something, sir. I was on my way to the rectory to report on our progress with the fresco."

The rector took a sip of brandy and poured a tot for Jonathan.

"I am afraid that I have been less than tolerant of your relationship with my

## For Dad On Father's Day

SO many happy memories
Light up this special day,
And safely stored within
   the mind
Can never fade away.

The loving thoughts, the
   caring touch,
The precious days we shared,
And though, sometimes, the
   words were few,
We knew how much
   you cared.

Though time and tide
   flow swiftly on
And years go slipping by,
The love we knew still
   grows, dear Dad,
For love can never die.

*– Iris Hesselden.*

daughter. For some while I have felt that marriage to Mr Cornwell would be in her best interests, and I was distressed when I saw my hopes being dashed. Now I am by no means so sure that I was right in my judgement."

"Mr Stanbrook, I am aware that I am a young man at the beginning of my career and that my resources are limited. But I have every hope of furthering my career. As for your daughter, I would wish her nothing but happiness and security."

"Generous words, Jonathan. I owe you a great deal."

Faye saw her opportunity.

"Then you will have no objection to Jonathan escorting me to the picnic, Father?"

"I am sure you will take good care of Faye," the rector said. "As to future assignations, well, we shall have to see."

\* \* \* \*

"I have been looking forward to this outing all the week, Faye," Jonathan said, leading her back through the churchyard and holding her hand.

"And so have I."

"I feel that your father is still unhappy about us."

"He is coming round slowly. Your courage this afternoon impressed him deeply."

Jonathan nodded uncertainly.

"Even so, I would rather he gave us his unguarded blessing."

"Oh, he will in due course, I feel sure. Come and look at the wonderful display of butterflies on the buddleia."

There were three Painted Ladies, a score of Tortoiseshells, a Small Blue, a Hairstreak and, poised on a flower, was one magnificent specimen.

"Look!" she said breathlessly, pointing to the large butterfly with velvet black wings bordered by white. "It's a Camberwell Beauty! So rare, delicate and lovely."

She was aware of a hand taking hers, of a voice not entirely steady.

"Rare, delicate and lovely, Faye. Those are the words that have been hovering on my lips all this last week."

She turned two green, teasing eyes on him.

"You have seen the Camberwell Beauty earlier this week?"

"No, Faye. It is you that I have seen. Every waking moment of the day."

FAYE woke to sunshine, the scent of honeysuckle drifting through the window and the sound of birdsong. Later, she slipped into her father's study.

"I am making my way to the parsonage field now. Jonathan is to meet me there."

"I shall join you shortly, Faye. I have a letter to finish first."

She suddenly felt an urge to go inside the church to see how work on the fresco was going. The interior smelled of stone dust, candle grease and ancient oak beams.

She walked over to the transept and stared upwards. She could just make out a further section that had been cleared, depicting Jonah being swallowed by a whale. The ladder stood invitingly against the scaffolding.

Holding the sides of the ladder, she cautiously made her way up, careful not to get her long dress tangled. At last she reached the narrow planks from which the stonemason did his work. She was peering closely at Jonah when there was a gliding sound, followed by a crash. Turning round, she saw to her horror that the ladder had slipped sideways and fallen to the ground. There she was, 25 feet up, standing on a narrow ledge scarcely eight inches wide!

Panic seized her and she stood stock still, terrified of falling.

"Help! Help!" she called. But nobody heard, for the walls were thick and everybody was at the picnic.

She closed her eyes, trying to shut out the frightening drop, and prayed with all her might to St Mary, the patron saint of the church. She had no idea how long she stood there, only that her muscles were cramped and her legs unsteady.

But the saint must have heard her, for the handle of the west door squeaked and Jonathan, after taking one look, tore across the aisle.

"Faye, my love, hold on! I'll be with you in an instant." She heard the scrape of wood on stone, the hurrying of footsteps on the rungs and then two strong arms half carried her down, shaken and frightened.

The rector glanced out of the study window and saw them returning. He rushed out, his face creased with worry.

"Faye, Jonathan, whatever has happened?"

A small voice answered.

"I did something very foolish and went into the church to look at the fresco. I climbed up and the ladder slipped."

"You were trapped on that narrow ledge, so high up?"

"Yes, Father. Jonathan rescued me. Had it been any longer I should have fainted and fallen."

Jonathan gently eased her into an armchair and kneeled down, stroking her hair.

"When she didn't turn up at the picnic I panicked. Nobody had seen a sign of her. I searched high and low, and then something drew me to the church."

"Saint Mary," Faye said softly. "I prayed that she would bring me help."

The Reverend Silas gave his daughter a long, loving hug. At that moment he realised that he had been wrong all along. What were land and money, compared to the gentleness and love this young man was showing to his daughter?

"I feel ashamed that I have been so blind to your virtues, Jonathan."

The young architect smiled.

"Does that mean that artists have been given a reprieve, sir?"

"It does indeed, my boy."

"And Father," Faye said with a hint of mischief in those green eyes, "does it mean that Jonathan has your blessing to court me?"

"That, too, my child. Jonathan has rescued me from a runaway trap and saved my daughter from a fall that could have been fatal. Not only that, he has shown himself to be caring and thoughtful. Can a better suitor be found for any young girl?"

Later on, they made their way to the church to offer a prayer of thanksgiving and there, with the bearded Noah looking sternly on and beneath the gaze of a curious giraffe, Jonathan kissed his loved one for the first time.

Faye's father smiled serenely and looked across to the chancel steps where he had joined so many couples in Holy Matrimony. Then he went into the vestry and drew the leather-bound marriage registers from the church safe and opened them.

Yes, there was still room for another entry. ▇

## Bimbo 1963

IT might have been the worst winter since 1946-47, but children could find plenty of cosy warmth in the first "Bimbo" annual. The friendly introduction, like that in the comics, was a letter to readers with a mixture of large, clearly printed words and pictures, so that little ones could have the satisfaction of "reading along" with Mummy or Daddy.

Featuring regular characters from the weekly comic, like Pussy Willow, the Teddy Bears and Baby Crockett, there were also new stories to read, puzzles to do, pictures to colour in and ideas for everyday fun, like making pictures with the buttons from Mummy's button box.

Once all the stories had been read, little readers had other favourites to occupy them that year. Enid Blyton published "Noddy And The Aeroplane", the 24th in her famous series featuring the behatted little character and his gnome friend, Big-Ears. And when reading was done for the day, Pedigree's new fashion doll, Sindy, would help to occupy many happy hours. Little brothers, for whom Sindy might have held less attraction, would perhaps have been more pleased to welcome the very first episode of "Doctor Who", shown for the first time on November 23, 1963. ■

*Illustration by Boni.*

# Picking Up
# The Pieces

## — by Em Barnard. —

**J**ENNY reached for the plastic rabbit head by its one ear and picked it off the dump. Clutching the little girl by the hand, she led her out through the gate of the steel-netted recycling bay in the corner of the Acorn Garden Centre where she worked. The youngster had become fractious, refusing to leave it.

After securing the bay's gate, Jenny set the smiling head snugly in a large terracotta pot. Broken in five pieces, the metre-high plastic statue, in red trousers and waistcoat and hugging a bunch of carrots, had been cast on to the pile of shattered pots beside a green bin for organic waste.

"There. Now you won't get your pretty dress dirty," she said to the child, ▶

thankful she hadn't cut herself.

"What's his name?" The child gave Jenny a bright look.

"Er, Peter," Jenny replied, searching for a frantic parent among those wandering around the outside display area. The warm sunshine had attracted many folk this May bank holiday weekend. "And what's your name?" she asked, attending to the child again.

"Izzy!" The call came from down the aisle as a man in dark T-shirt, jeans and trainers twisted through folk towards them. He grasped the child's hand. "You mustn't run off like that, Izzy!"

"I came to see Peter. He wants to come home and stay with Pixie."

"I told you earlier, Izzy, he's too broken." To Jenny he explained, "She has a plastic one very much the same at home."

"I had two," Izzy confided. "But Dixie went to heaven to help Mummy and Jesus in his garden. Pixie misses him an awful lot."

"He was stolen," the man said in a quiet undertone. "We'll find her a friend soon, Izzy," he said more loudly, then turned to Jenny again. "Thank you." With a smile and a nod, he tugged his daughter on.

"But we must take Peter!" As Izzy tugged back he hefted her in his arms and strode on. She began to whine, hand reaching back in a grasping motion.

Once they'd gone Jenny returned the rabbit head to the bay, propping it at an angle on top of the crock heap. He smiled back at her through lively brown eyes in a fur-sculptured face.

She understood Izzy's heartache, for she'd been collecting damaged animal ornaments since she was a child. Tim, the boy next door, had helped repair them. She'd begun collecting when he had repaired a stone gnome with a broken hat they'd found on an allotment dump.

THE following day Jenny saw Izzy's father with Tim, now her manager, beside the recycling bay. They seemed in dispute. The father swung away and marched down the aisle.

As he came her way, Jenny called a cheerful "Good morning." He gave her a tight smile and nod as he strode past.

Jenny sighed, disappointed he hadn't remembered her. She remembered his hazel eyes and warming smile. She caught Tim's arm as he walked past.

"Is there a problem?" she asked.

"No. He wanted that broken rabbit, but I told him it was against policy, nor were we getting any more in."

Later that morning Jenny was in the bay tipping rubbish.

"OK, I'll try to take you home," she said, feeling the rabbit's smile on her. "But the rule is I can only take small items, and I can't exactly shove you under my arm."

At lunchtime, Jenny sat on her usual seat in the park opposite the garden centre eating tuna sandwiches. It was active with families this bank holiday

84

Monday, but her mind was fixed on Peter Rabbit.

She'd thought about how to get him to her car, and was now thinking how nice it would be, once he was repaired, to hand him to Izzy and see the child's face light up. But even as she pictured the moment, there in the background was the child's father, and it was his smile she yearned to see again.

At twenty-seven she'd not met anyone other than Tim who had touched her heart. She and Tim still saw each other often, but in friendship only.

"Hello, lady. Have you still got Peter Rabbit?"

Jenny returned from her daydream, surprised to meet Izzy's hope-filled eyes as she ran up to her.

"Hello, Izzy." She smiled as the child's father walked up.

"Izzy, he's much too broken to repair. Isn't that right, Jenny?" he said, picking up on her name badge.

"Your daddy would cut his fingers on the sharp pieces," Jenny agreed.

"No, he wouldn't. He fits windows, and glass is much sharper than Peter."

"Why don't you go and look at the ducks, Izzy?" her dad suggested.

As his daughter ran off to see the ducks waddling on to the grass, he sat beside Jenny.

"I'm Greg. I'm sorry if we're being a nuisance to you," he said in his warm-toned voice. "Isabel's mother died two years ago and the rabbits were her last gift to Izzy. I did ask your manager this morning if I could take it, but he said no. I could have repaired it for her. When Dixie was stolen a couple of weeks ago, I told Izzy he'd gone to stay with her mummy. I thought it best to bring Pixie into the conservatory in case the thieves returned." His gaze flicked to his daughter.

Jenny regarded him. There was strength in his leanness, accentuated by the cling of his T-shirt and the long, practical fingers.

"Listen, Greg, if you could back your car up to the customer collection gate at the rear around closing time, I'll get it out to you."

"I couldn't ask you to do that!"

"The lorry's coming first thing tomorrow to empty the bay, and I was going to take him anyway." She told him of her collection and that she was allowed the cast-offs from the bay. "So I'd like to do this for Izzy."

"Thank you, Jenny. It's Izzy's birthday in a month, which is another reason I wanted the rabbit," he told her conspiratorially, his face so close she could smell his soapy aroma. "I won't mention it to her. I'll leave her with my mum this evening."

\*　\*　\*　\*

Jenny hurried down to the recycling bay with her wheelbarrow. It was full of limp greenery as a cover for her manoeuvres. Her heart pounded; she hoped she wouldn't collide with Tim, or Mr Mowles, their senior manager.

She reached for the head with its one ear, sure it was smiling wider at its fortune. Then the four pieces that made up the body. She covered them with a thick green thatch before searching for the missing ear and foot. She spotted the ear and reached for it.

"What are you doing, Jenny?"

Briefly she closed her eyes, then stepped from the broken pots and faced Mr Mowles, her hand sliding into the pocket of her jacket.

"Just tidying for the lorry tomorrow morning."

"Well, leave it. I need to get away early tonight."

In the car park Jenny hurried to the rear, where she saw Greg leaning against an estate car.

"I'm sorry. I couldn't get it."

"That's OK. I should never have let you try. I wondered, though, if you'd care to come out for a meal?"

"Wait!" Jenny dashed off, having spied Tim getting into his car. "Tim, I need your key to the rear gates of the recycling bay."

"Why?" One foot on the tarmac, he glanced at Greg. "What are you up to, Jen? That's the man I turned away this morning."

"I told him I'd get him the rabbit."

He caught a laugh in his throat, astonished.

"You're not serious?"

"I've taken broken ornaments before."

"Yes, small ones for yourself."

"It is for me, as far as anyone's concerned. Look, all the pieces are on the wheelbarrow in the bay. I was hoping to wheel it out before we closed but Mr Mowles caught me."

"Jen . . ."

"Please, Tim." She glanced at Greg.

"Once he's driven off you'll never see him again," Tim warned her.

"Wrong. He's just asked me out, I think. But I really want to do this for Izzy." She jutted her chin defiantly. "If you don't help me, I'll be here first thing in the morning when the lorry arrives."

He held up the key, still on the bunch. She popped a kiss on his cheek.

"Don't look so worried, Tim. I'll be back in no time."

Five minutes later Greg shut the rear door of his car.

"Thanks, Jenny. Izzy will be over the moon! You sure you won't get into trouble?" He glanced at Tim, leaning against his car.

"Oh, Tim's OK. We go way back. Now, there's a foot and an ear missing. The ear is in my locker. I can bring it to the pond tomorrow lunchtime. Maybe by then I'll have found the foot!"

Jenny hurried back to Tim. Dropping the keys in his palm, she popped a kiss on his cheek again for being so helpful.

## Happy Birthday

CHERRY blossom clusters
Shine against the sky,
As swallows, swifts and martins
Tirelessly fly by.
Cows and sheep meander,
Munching as they go,
While the willow branches
Sway gently to and fro.
Little lambs frisk happily
In meadows lush and green,
To create a happy atmosphere,
Calm, tranquil and serene.
A dewy, daisy-dappled lawn
Backdrops the joyful view,
With phlox and stocks and
   hollyhocks
And dainty feverfew.
So sunny May has paved the way
And put the scene in tune,
To wish a happy birthday
To her brand-new sister, June . . .

*– Brian H. Gent.*

Then she hurried over to her own car, acknowledging Greg with a lift of a hand as he drove past.

NERVOUSLY, Jenny sat on her usual seat watching the ducks, glancing now and then in each direction for Greg. But it was Tim who marched towards her.

"What are you doing here?" she growled, jumping to her feet.

"Just passing, Jen," he replied. "I'm meeting someone in the bandstand."

"Sorry, Tim. I'm a bit edgy. He's late."

"He'd be a fool not to fall for your charms."

His quip brought a smile from her. He winked and walked on.

Moments later Greg approached.

"Hello!" she said brightly, tugging her gaze from Tim.

"You have the ear for me?"

She rooted in her shoulder bag.

"No sign of the missing foot, I'm afraid. But I'll keep a lookout."

"I'll patch it."

"Is Izzy OK?"

"She's at nursery school." He accepted the ear with a smile, but his eyes were troubled. "Well, thanks for all you've done for Izzy and me." He took a breath and Jenny thought he was about to ask her out again, but with a nod and a smile he turned away.

Jenny looked after him, disappointed.

The next day, checking stock with Tim, she was trying to remember what she had heard.

"I'm sure he asked me out when we were in the car park. But he was so distant yesterday at the pond."

"Maybe he had other things on his mind, Jen."

"You mean he didn't fancy me?" She smiled at Tim.

He grinned but Jenny picked up an undercurrent of unease in it.

"Something bothering you, Tim?"

"I've met a girl. I didn't like to mention it while you were upset about Greg."

Jen clutched his forearm, beaming.

"Oh, Tim, I'm OK. So, who is she? Could she be the one?" Jenny arched her eyebrows mischievously. She wanted Tim to find happiness.

✳    ✳    ✳    ✳

A few days later, Jenny was so delighted at what she spied behind the green bin that she grasped it and hurried to find Tim. She opened her hand and showed him the rabbit's foot.

"Didn't he say he'd patch it, Jen?"

"Yes, but he might come in to see if I've found it." She slumped as he gave her a doubting look. "It's a chance in a million."

"Do you have a contact number for him?"

"Didn't get that far. He might be back. Meanwhile, I'll hang on to the rabbit's foot. After all, it is supposed to be a good-luck charm!"

TWO weeks later, on Friday morning, Jenny turned from tidying pots of perennials to see the smiling face of Greg.

"Hi. I've an invitation for you to Izzy's party." He held out a pink envelope. "I need to apologise for my behaviour at the pond the other week. I thought you and Tim were romantically involved."

"Me and Tim?"

"He saw me yesterday when I came in and approached me. Or, should I say, challenged me!" He chuckled. "It seems I got the wrong end of the stick when I saw you kiss him in the car park and at the pond. I thought the two of you were an item, but Tim told me you're just close friends."

Jenny groaned.

"We do kiss. It's just an affectionate gesture between us. Did Tim tell you I found the rabbit's foot?"

"He told me. But I've moulded one ready to glue on. I came for cement to weigh Peter down, as he's quite light. Izzy has no idea. Anyway, as this invite is coming a hundred per cent from me, will you accept?"

Jenny reached for the invitation.

"I'd love to."

T
HE door was opened in answer to Jenny's press on the bell by Izzy in a pink sparkly dress.

"Hello," Greg said from behind her. "Remember this lady, Izzy?"

"Have you mended Peter?" the little girl asked excitedly.

"No, but I have an important piece of him for you," Jenny replied as Greg led her into the lounge full of kids and adults. They gathered round as she handed Izzy a small box. Izzy tore away the pink metallic paper and opened the lid.

She stared at the plastic foot then pouted in disappointment.

Jenny dropped to her haunches.

"A rabbit's foot is a magical thing, Izzy, if you close your eyes and wish hard enough," she whispered in Izzy's ear. "So if you were to say, 'please make Peter mended and standing beside Pixie', then it just might happen!"

Izzy gaped.

"Let's get all your friends to close their eyes and wish, too," Jenny suggested.

As they did so, and with the adults smiling knowingly, Jenny put the lidded box in Izzy's hands. Then while the kids wished, Greg sneaked away with the foot that Jenny had passed him.

"Now, Izzy," Jenny said, "open the box. If the foot's missing, then your wish has been granted."

Izzy peered inside.

"It's gone!"

"Then Peter must be in the conservatory!"

But Izzy was already pushing through the adults, gathering a train of children as she ran on.

"He's here! Peter's here!" Izzy ran up to the statue.

After the excitement had calmed down, Greg took Jenny aside.

"Phew! That was a bit hairy."

He gave a thumbs-up sign to some mates who'd struggled in with Peter from the garden shed while they were all in the lounge.

"So, will you come out for a meal with me one evening so I can thank you properly?"

"Me, too!" Izzy ran up and clutched Jenny.

Laughing, Jenny caught Greg's smile, and felt it wouldn't be long before he was taking her in his arms, too. ■

## Iona, Inner Hebrides

**IONA ABBEY** is one of Scotland's most historic and sacred sites. The abbey was founded by St Columba and his Irish followers in AD 563. A celebrated focus for Christian pilgrimage, Iona retains its spiritual atmosphere and remains an enduring symbol of worship.

The abbey church was restored at the beginning of the 20th century, whilst work on restoring the living accommodation began in 1938, following the foundation of the Iona Community. Today, the Iona Community continues the tradition of worship first established by St Columba 1,450 years ago.

Look out for Reilig Odhráin – the little cemetery beside Sràid nam Marbh, "the street of the dead", where many ancient Scottish kings were laid to rest. The abbey graveyard also contains the graves of kings from Ireland, Norway and France. Among the numerous kings buried there are Malcolm II, King of Scotland, Duncan, King of Scotland, Macbeth, King of Scotland, Upsak Hakon, Norse King of the Isles and Somerled, Lord of the Isles. ■

*Illustration by Kirk Houston/Thinkstockphotos.*

# Side By Side

### — by *Catherine Howarth*. —

TOM caught sight of Margaret watching him through the sitting-room window and he waved to her, before dashing in a minute later, holding a car magazine over his head as a makeshift umbrella. Then he sat down beside her on the sofa with his customary grin.

"You all right, love?" he said, eyebrows raised, as he put an arm round her shoulders.

Margaret nodded and smiled as she rested her head against him.

"I was just thinking about the day we first spoke to each other, at the bus stop."

"Ah, you're going back a bit. The bus stop; the most romantic place in the country!" He laughed. "Well, for me, anyway."

He sat up and looked at her with sincere blue eyes and squeezed her hand.

"We should go away, just us. Do you fancy a holiday?"

Margaret was surprised; Tom wasn't at all fond of trips abroad.

"It hasn't been just the two of us for a long time, has it?" Tom continued.

When Margaret thought about it, they'd barely managed even a day out together recently.

91

They'd made plans to, of course, and Sunday mornings usually began with an optimistic suggestion for a drive in the country, or a drive to the sea where they could enjoy a spot of lunch.

Instead, what happened every time was that Tom would go out to start the car and find that it had no intention of going anywhere. She'd see him from the window, doing his best to kick-start the engine into life, and then he would wander in again much later, oblivious to the time, covered in oil and grease.

"Right, love, we're all set!" he'd announce cheerfully.

Of course, it was too late to go anywhere by then . . .

"A holiday would be great. I'd love to go away!"

As Margaret passed him his sandwich, her tummy gave a little flutter of anticipation.

"We never do anything on the spur of the moment. Let's sort something out and go soon!" Tom said, planting a loving kiss on her cheek.

THE next day, Margaret was browsing the brochure selection at the local travel agent's when one of the covers caught her eye. *Driving Holidays Around Britain.*

The cover depicted a couple on a classic motorcycle, riding along a winding road through the mountains, the woman's pink scarf fluttering behind her in the summer breeze. It was an attractive-looking scene, and with a slight sinking feeling she knew that this would probably be Tom's idea of a perfect holiday.

Absent-mindedly her hands touched her own pink scarf, a birthday gift from him. Her dreams of sun-drenched beaches and of sipping sangria on the terrace began to fade.

She thought of the beautifully restored motorcycle Tom had in his garden workshop. She'd never seen him ride it and she wasn't sure she would ever have the nerve to climb on the back of it.

Her memory flitted through their previous family holidays as she collected several brochures. There had been the Algarve, Spain, Majorca, and if she was honest with herself she knew that Tom had gone along for his family's sake; he disliked flying and warmer climates didn't appeal. His favourite holiday, she knew, had been spent in Cornwall, when the children were small.

Perhaps she could have been more thoughtful – they could have tried a caravan holiday once in a while. Maybe she had been too busy thinking of the children and their preferences.

Now, Margaret was thinking so much about all the choices she'd seen in the different brochures that she found she couldn't make up her mind. It was to be a special holiday, just for the two of them.

She arrived home and put the brochures down on the coffee table, then busied herself with making dinner.

"I'm back!"

Tom greeted her cheerfully and planted a warm kiss on her cheek.

"Oh, you got some, too?"

Margaret laughed in surprise. She was astonished that the brochures he was holding were all for winter sun holidays. So Tom was expecting to travel far afield.

Later, as they looked through the brochures together, Margaret nudged him.

"I thought your idea of a perfect holiday would be to go on a tour with that old bike of yours!"

"As if I would do that to you, love! My youngest girl has just flown the nest – I don't want to send the oldest one packing as well!"

"Less of the old. I'm younger than you!" Margaret protested. "But what about flying? I know you don't like planes."

Tom shook his head and held up a hand.

"It's going to be fine; we're going to have a great holiday!"

Tom pointed out a villa in Spain that took his fancy.

"I'll phone and book tomorrow, then." Margaret clapped her hands.

The following afternoon, Margaret sat deep in thought as Helen, the helpful travel agent, spoke to her. All the time she was listening to the itinerary details there was something niggling at the back of her mind.

Just Tom and me now.

Had they both been so busy with work and family that they had forgotten what it meant to be together? She wanted that feeling of closeness again, like when they had first met . . .

"So I'll just confirm all that and then we're sorted." Helen coughed politely.

Margaret looked up. She bit her lip. Was she doing the right thing for both of them? At last she nodded.

Helen printed off the details and handed them to Margaret with a smile.

✳   ✳   ✳   ✳

Tom was making a cup of tea when Margaret arrived home.

"Is that it?"

Margaret nodded and smiled just as the phone rang. It was Kate, calling from university.

"Mum, it's brilliant here, and my room-mate Clare is great. I don't feel like I'm on my own. I'm so relieved there's someone to chat to! Are you both OK?"

"Yes, we're fine. Missing you, of course, but Dad and I are going to take a little holiday!"

"Great idea. Have a lovely time! Must go, my phone battery is fading. Love you!"

"We love you, too!"

Margaret concentrated on preparing for the holiday. She was so excited. She'd treated herself to new trousers and a matching jacket. She'd also made sure that the camera was packed.

The beach towels, sunglasses and sun cream were in a neat pile in the corner. She'd asked Julie from next door to keep an eye on the house and the milk delivery was cancelled.

Finally, their bags were packed and they were ready to leave.

"All set?" Tom grinned as he came indoors to collect the bags.

Margaret nodded, suddenly feeling a little uneasy.

Tom held her tight.

"It's going to be great, love," he whispered, gazing into her eyes. "Thank you for doing this. I can't wait to set off!"

With those words, her unease melted away as he picked up her bag and she followed him downstairs.

It was a cool morning and her new boots felt strangely comforting wrapped around her feet. She was aware that she was beaming like a love-struck teenager as she waved to Julie, who was standing at the gate smiling in surprise.

"You're a braver girl than me, Margaret! And don't you look great in that new jacket?"

Julie laughed as Margaret took a deep breath and climbed a little shakily on to the back of the motorcycle, wearing her new padded blue and black bike trousers and matching jacket, her small luggage bag strapped safely to the back carrier.

"You take good care of her, Tom!" Julie called as she waved them off.

He would, Margaret thought as she put her arms around his waist and held him tight. He always had, and he always would.

This would be a different holiday, that was for sure.

The day before, she had confessed to Tom that she'd been a little bit sneaky. She hadn't booked the Spanish villa, as he'd thought, but instead a number of guesthouses across the country. The look of delighted surprise on his face and that broad grin when she told him was well worth forgoing her trip to Spain.

Tom always wanted to make her happy, and Margaret had felt it was about time she did something that made him happy, too. After all, that was what their life together was all about, whatever they were going through.

As they rode away, Margaret knew she wouldn't worry about the cold or the rain, or whether the silly old machine might conk out before they got to the first roundabout.

She had seen Tom's eyes shine with happiness, just like when they first met. They were entering a new phase, just the two of them, and a warm feeling of complete contentment flooded over her, as it dawned on her that this could well be phase one all over again. ■

94

*Illustration by Mandy Dixon/Thinkstockphotos.*

# An Englishman Abroad

## *by Paula Gregory.*

WE were visiting the Louvre, my sister and I. It was the last day of my holiday in Paris and she thought I should absorb a bit of culture before I went home. Louisa was working as a translator in France and had invited me to stay for the week. I'd had a wonderful time – meeting her friends, eating at her favourite cafés, even improving my French. And, of course, I'd been introduced to Étienne, her boyfriend. He was lovely and I could see how much he cared for Louisa. Even the way he pronounced her name made me smile.

Still, here I was in the most romantic place on earth but I hadn't a scrap of romance in my own life. In fact, I'd just left a long relationship with my first serious boyfriend. We'd been together since senior school and Desmond and I had finally admitted to ourselves that we were just a habit, not the enduring passion I'd hoped for. Still, we'd parted friends just before our families began hinting at engagements and more serious stuff.

"I liked Desmond, Elaine," Louisa said when I told her over the phone.

"But I never thought he was right for you. He was much too serious."

It was true, he didn't even like to be called "Des".

"Come over and stay for a bit. Get a different perspective on your life."

* * * *

We were just approaching the shining glass pyramid at the Louvre when we heard English voices and saw a group of four men with a camera.

"Here's a couple of likely girls," a voice said. "Why don't you try your technique on them, Kit? At this rate we'll never meet any *mademoiselles*!"

Louisa had certainly absorbed French chic, and had smartened my fashion sense during the time I'd been with her. No doubt that was why they'd mistaken us for locals.

A tall rangy man with hair like a lion's mane approached us with a grin. He was holding the camera towards us.

"*S'il vous plaît, mademoiselles*," he said. "Would you, er, *voulez-vous* take a – *une* – photograph of us together? *Oui*?"

"Eh, our Louisa, I think this bloke is trying to sell us his camera!" I said in my broadest accent. "I don't think it's much cop, do you? He's probably nicked it off a tourist. What do you think?"

The man called Kit started to laugh. It was a deep, rumbling laugh that was so catching that soon all six of us were laughing.

"So, where do you girls come from?" Kit asked.

"Haslingden," I said. "It's a little town in Lancashire," I added just in case he had no idea.

"I know where Haslingden is," he said. "We're all from Preston!"

I should have recognised his accent.

"Small world," Louisa said.

"My sister's living in Paris," I explained. "I've been staying with her. She's fluent in French."

"I didn't think much of your efforts with the language," Louisa said, laughing.

"What were you up to?"

"We took you for a couple of French girls. We've been trying to meet up with some locals all week," his friend said. "Kit thought up this plan to ask girls to take a photo of us all so we could get talking to them. Most of them refused and were a bit snooty when they saw us scruffy lot. We've been camping outside Paris and we thought we'd soak up a bit of culture before we went home."

"We've just queued up to see the Mona Lisa," one of the others said. "But to be honest I don't know what all the fuss is about."

"Philistine!" the other three chorused and we all set off laughing again.

"Elaine and I are just about to go in and see her," Louisa told them. "Would you like us to take your photo before we go?"

"Why not." Kit grinned. "And perhaps we can take one of you, too. If you

96

give me your e-mail address I can send it on."

So we posed in various lively groups, then we exchanged names and I wrote my e-mail address on the back of the catalogue that Kit had.

That would be the last I heard of him, I knew. The catalogue would be thrown in a bin, the photographs of Liz and me deleted from the memory of the camera. I liked Kit and we'd got on well together, but we were passing strangers.

Next day I said goodbye at the airport. I kissed Étienne on both cheeks and hugged my sister, so sorry to be going home.

"Come back soon, Elaine," she said. "I'll miss you."

Promising I would, I left for home.

WE had a visitor while you were away," Mum said as she and Dad drove me home from the airport.

"Who was that?" I asked, intrigued by her arch smile.

"Desmond called round to see you," she told me. "He seemed disappointed you weren't in. I told him you were in Paris. I think he's missing you."

"Oh!" I said, surprised to say the least. Desmond and I had parted on good terms, but I couldn't understand why he'd called to see me.

Suddenly I was faced with a dilemma. What would I say if he asked me to go back with him? I missed him, of course. We'd been a couple for ages, and it felt strange being single. But was that a reason to get back together?

I thought of Paris, and wondered how I'd have felt with Desmond by my side. Would we have fallen in love again, surrounded by the romance of the city? I suspected he'd have felt happier in the Lake District or Scotland, just as romantic but too familiar, their beauty taken for granted. Like our relationship had become.

"He said he'd call again when you were home."

My mother liked Desmond and was sorry that we'd parted. She'd been happy with the thought that I'd marry and settle down near home, since Louisa had found love abroad and was likely to end up living in France.

"Perhaps you could give him a ring when you get home," she tried.

"I'll wait until he calls again."

That might give me time to think.

\* \* \* \*

But next day, after I'd put all my washing in the machine and opened up my e-mails, I got another surprise. Among my messages there was one from Kit!

I opened it to find smiling pictures of myself, Louise and all the others larking about in front of the Louvre. I smiled, and realised it was the first time I'd smiled since I heard about Desmond's visit.

*I keep thinking about you,* Kit wrote. *I hung around outside the Louvre for ages hoping you'd come out but the others dragged me away in the end. I*

▶

*hope we can meet up some time. Please say yes.*

I didn't hesitate to reply.

*Love the pictures – love to see you again*, I wrote back and added my address and phone number.

I took a deep breath and pressed *send*.

Exactly half an hour later the doorbell rang.

"Someone here to see you, Elaine!" my mother called as she answered the door.

I didn't recognise Kit for a moment. He'd had his hair cut and wore a respectable shirt and trousers, instead of a creased T-shirt and jeans. He stood grinning in the hallway.

"You said I could come, so I didn't think you'd mind," he said, looking a little uncertain for a moment.

Never in a million years would Desmond have done something so impulsive. My heart skipped a beat at seeing Kit's cheery smiling face.

"Do you fancy coming out for a walk?" I asked, keen to escape Mum's watchful eye. "There's a little park near here."

He turned to me before we'd even left the garden gate.

"This may sound daft, but I told my mates that you were the girl I was going to marry."

I laughed.

"We'd better wait and see. I don't know if you've got any weird habits – and you don't know about mine!"

"Oh, I've got loads, but think of the fun you'll have finding them out. I won't mention the kipper juggling just yet."

People smiled at us as we ran, hand in hand, to the park, laughing like idiots. I sat on a bench to catch my breath and we sat and talked for ages.

Like me, Kit led quite an ordinary life with a sensible job in an insurance office, and lived at home with his parents. But Kit made everything sound so much fun.

It was nearly teatime when my mobile rang and Mum asked if we were coming home for something to eat.

"Tell her we'll get fish and chips and eat them out somewhere," Kit suggested. "I don't want to put her to any trouble."

So that was what we did. We drove to a beauty spot in the hills nearby and looked over the valley as we ate fish and chips with our fingers.

"Next time I'll take you somewhere posh," Kit promised, feeding me his last chip.

Our first kiss tasted of salt and vinegar, but it felt wonderful to me.

He drove me home as the light faded. I didn't want the day to end.

Back home Mum had "just thrown" some of her delicious scones together, and she managed to get in a few questions while we drank hot tea.

I waved Kit off with a promise that we'd meet at the weekend. I could hardly wait. As I lay in bed that night, the sensible part of my brain kept telling me that my thing with Kit could be all part of an illusion that could disappear in a puff of smoke. But the fluffy bit of brain told me firmly that it didn't matter one bit. I'd had a lovely romantic encounter that I wouldn't ever forget, and with a bit of luck I'd be having plenty more.

NEXT day there was a knock at the door, and I opened it to find Desmond.

"Hi, Elaine," he said, looking so sad that my heart nearly went out to him again.

"You'd better come in," I said.

Mum greeted him and disappeared into the kitchen.

"How have you been?"

"I expect your mum told you I'd called?" he said at the exact same moment. I nodded.

"I intended to ask if you fancied getting back together," he said quietly. "But I saw you in the park yesterday."

"Oh!" I hadn't been aware of anyone I knew watching us.

"You looked happy," he went on with a sad smile.

"That was Kit," I explained. "He's quite mad, but I like him."

"Then I'm glad for you." Desmond kissed my cheek. "If it doesn't work out, think about what I was going to suggest."

I squeezed his arm.

"I hope you find someone nice, Desmond. Someone to make you happy."

\*　\*　\*　\*

I heard Desmond got married to a girl we both knew at school.

The fluffy part of my brain was quite right. Kit and I continue to have our romantic encounters. We're still enthralled with each other, despite the misgivings of my parents. We'll never be rich, but we're happy. There's never a dull moment with Kit.

You can guess where we're going for our honeymoon. Paris, of course. Louisa and Étienne have offered us their flat while they come and visit my parents in Britain.

"Marry in haste, repent at leisure," Mum mutters. But I'll take my chances. I feel so right and sure about my love for Kit.

We plan to visit the Louvre again, and this time we'll be able to share our enjoyment. Perhaps we'll commandeer some bewildered tourist to take a photograph of us together. It can go in the album, along with those mad photos taken on the first day we met.

Kit and I were passing strangers, hopelessly romantic in a most romantic city. The spark of our love was born that day. But it was nourished and it grew, fed on fish and chips in a small Lancashire town. ■

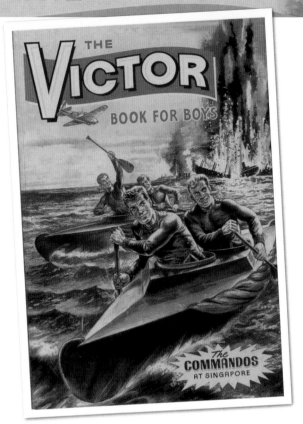

## Victor 1964

AS the Sixties progressed, the technological revolution in communications began to make itself felt. The pirate radio station, Radio Caroline, began broadcasting, heralding an explosion in the growth of commercial radio stations. In the same year, the iconic Post Office Tower building in London was completed (though it was not officially opened until 1965). On completion, the structure, now known as the BT Tower, became the tallest building in the city, a title it retained until 1980. It is still a major communications hub in the UK.

The "white heat of technology" referred to by the then prime minister, Harold Wilson, in a speech the previous year, was reflected in the content of the first copy of "The Victor Book For Boys", published in 1964.

A series on "Mechanical Marvels" enthralled young readers, with the gyroscope that was inspired by the balancing mechanism of a bumble bee, and a miniature camera that could fit inside a wrist watch. With a mix of stories about snipers in wartime, jungle explorers, intrepid Mounties and a plucky welding apprentice who just happened to run for Britain, "The Victor Book For Boys" was something no young chap would want to be without! ■

The
COMMANDOS

*Illustration by Stephanie Axtell.*

# That First Date

## — *by Cilla Moss.* —

I WAS waiting in a café on the high street. I couldn't remember ever being so nervous – at least, not since my first date with my husband. He'd even commented on it as I got dressed and asked him how I looked.

"Were you this bad when you were getting ready for our first date?"

"I was a wreck," I assured him. "My hands were shaking so much, I burned my neck with my hair tongs."

But the prospect of meeting Maddie for coffee had me in even more of a tizz. I kept checking my watch. She was five minutes late. Had she forgotten?

She'd invited me for coffee after our last yoga class, but I didn't imagine it meant half as much to her as it did to me. It seemed like Maddie was always rushing from one engagement to another – she had no spare time.

My life was so quiet in comparison. We'd moved to Wales from Leeds a little over six months ago with Keith's engineering job. As a private music teacher, I could work anywhere, but it also meant most of my acquaintances were small children. Being terribly shy didn't help.

I'd persuaded myself to give in to my nerves and scarper when I saw her arrive. She was carrying a large shoulder bag and smiled charmingly at the man who held the door for her. I envied her that easy friendliness with strangers. The first time we met she'd found out from me in about thirty seconds that I was new to the area and what I did for a living. We'd talked a few times since, and eventually she'd made the invitation when we were both walking to our cars after class.

"Do you fancy meeting for coffee next week?"

So here we were.

"Hi, Delia!" She greeted me so warmly I forgot all my worries. In seconds she'd collected her own coffee and joined me at the table.

"I'm sorry if I kept you waiting," she said. "I had to drop off my daughter at my mother's house, then pick up some samples for work . . ." I knew she worked as a freelance interior designer.

"It's no problem. Sounds like you've had a busy day."

"No more hectic than usual." She paused suddenly. "I guess you must be wondering why I wanted to meet up," she said eventually. "The thing is . . . I was hoping for some professional advice."

So this hadn't been a social invitation, after all.

"My daughter, Josie, is five, and I was thinking about music lessons."

"Five is a great age to start," I said. "I teach piano and violin, but I can recommend some other teachers if you had a different instrument in mind."

"I was hoping for something like a choir or a music group. She's a quiet girl, and she's finding it hard to make friends at school."

I could relate to Josie!

"I'm afraid I don't run any group lessons. But have you thought about one of those stage schools, where they teach performing arts on weekends?"

"Oh. I didn't realise. I hope you don't think I've wasted your time."

"Of course not. I'm just sorry I can't be more help." It seemed like our coffee date might be over almost before it had begun, and the afternoon suddenly felt like a damp squib.

"To be honest, I know how Josie feels," I murmured with a sigh. "I always had trouble making friends at school. Some people make it look so easy."

"Don't they?" Maddie agreed. "I'm envious of people like that."

I stared at her. Wasn't she one of those people?

"I've lost touch with lots of my old friends," Maddie said. "Life moves into new phases. And then, being so busy, you don't realise . . ."

I looked at her suddenly wistful face. Maybe we weren't going to see much of each other after today, but I could still try to be a good friend to her.

"If you've got a few minutes, we could walk to the library. They'll have information about music classes and children's activities."

## Musings From A Maze

I WOULDN'T really say I'm lost – I'm simply not-quite-sure.
It all looks so familiar – did I pass this way before?
And now as I start turning, just to check which way I came,
It's perfectly perplexing, for each pathway looks the same.
If only I'd brought breadcrumbs, I would leave a little trail,
But outside it looked easy, and I thought I couldn't fail.
I rushed in bright and breezy, but I now regret my haste –
Though still I wouldn't say I'm lost, I'm certainly misplaced.
But am I down and daunted? No – despite so many ways,
Confused, bemused, bewildered, I will get out of this maze!

*– Maggie Ingall.*

"Are you sure?" She looked doubtful. "It's not very interesting for you."

"I wouldn't mind finding out myself. And they might have brochures for the new theatre season in Cardiff."

Maddie brightened.

"I love musicals, don't you?"

We left the café and stepped into the bright day, chatting about our favourite shows. Maddie paused and raised her face to the sun.

"It's so nice to have a moment to enjoy the day," she said, then laughed. "There I go again. My mother's always scolding me for going on about how busy I am. She says it makes people feel I haven't got time for them.

"It's not as if I'm doing anything especially important," she went on. "I'm usually just trying to keep things running smoothly. It's a lack of organisation, probably. I mean, look at this." She patted her bag. "I'm actually carrying my dry-cleaning around with me!"

At the library we spent a few happy minutes collecting brochures and leaflets.

We were still leafing through them when we stepped back outside, chatting about a local amateur dramatic production of "Chicago".

"Bronwyn Jones is playing Velma Kelly – can you imagine?" She giggled. "In stockings and heels. She's the mayor!"

▶ We started to walk away from the high street, enjoying the sunshine and the view, still talking.

I told her how I'd really fallen for the landscape here. For her part she told me how she had moved to London for work when she was younger and starting her career, but had been so miserable in a big city she'd had to come home.

The conversation came easier as we found things we had in common. There weren't many silences between us, but if ever we got stuck we started to talk about Josie again.

"I hope she'll be all right," Maddie said eventually.

I could feel the afternoon winding down. As the light began to fade and the air cooled, we started back to our cars.

"I told her she had to try to talk to people and not to be so shy," she went on, "but I realised I wasn't exactly setting her a good example."

"But you're great at talking to people," I protested.

"Maybe. But . . ." She fidgeted a bit. "Oh, it sounds stupid, but it's been a long time since I made a new friend."

"I know what you mean. It's like you get out of practice as you get older."

"It feels like primary school all over again." She laughed sheepishly.

Was it possible Maddie was shy? The thought made me brave.

"Well," I said, "thanks for today. I know you just wanted to talk about Josie, but it's been nice to have some girl time."

She beamed at me.

"I enjoyed it, too."

I mustered my courage.

"And if you ever feel like meeting for coffee again . . ."

"Oh, I'd really like to!" Maddie said. "And . . ." She coloured slightly. "It wasn't really to talk about Josie that I wanted to meet up. I just didn't really know how to start the conversation. I hope you don't mind."

She stuffed her leaflets and brochures into her bag.

"Hey," she said, something catching her eye, "they're running a salsa class at the community centre! I've always wanted to try that."

"Me, too. But Keith won't go and I just don't have the nerve to go by myself."

"*We* should go!" she exclaimed.

"Yes, why not?" I said, just as quickly.

"Let me give you my phone number."

"Oh, I've left my phone in the car!"

So I wrote my number in Biro across her wrist.

"Just like primary school," she said, smiling.

"Just like primary school," I echoed.

And it was. Like one of those giddy, happy days when you come home with a new best friend. ■

*Illustration by David McAllister.*

# The Red Car

## *by Suzanne Ross Jones.*

**W**ILLIAM frowned as he pushed open the rusty garage door. It seemed wrong to be doing this on Father's Day. But when his dad had brought up the subject over lunch William hadn't been able to resist having a look to see how the car had fared in the years it had been locked away.

The Triumph Stag had been brand new and gleaming red the first time William had seen it. His father had been so proud as he'd brought his family outside to have a look. Even though that was nearly 40 years ago, William remembered his father's words.

"One day, son, this car will come to you. You have to promise me you'll look after it!"

For years it had been the family's pride as he and his dad had driven

▶

105

around the countryside on day trips. Those memories brought a lump to his throat as he looked at the car. Especially as that long-promised day had arrived, and the car was now his.

"Sad, isn't it?" His mum had joined him at the doorway, peering over his shoulder into the dusty and dingy old garage.

"Very sad." To see the car in its faded state was heartbreaking.

"You're not going to take it, are you?"

"Dad wants me to have it."

"But look at it! And what will Pam say if you take it home?"

He shrugged.

"If it's in the garage, out of the way, then I'm sure Pam won't mind."

"I could just ring the scrapyard," his mum offered. "Get them to send someone around to collect it."

William shook his head.

"That would break Dad's heart."

"It would," she conceded. "He kept meaning to do something about it, but it's unbelievable how quickly the years have flown by. And now we're downsizing this huge place for a bungalow, we've no space for it."

"OUR old new car," Pam said as the lorry arrived with the car. "It'll just sit in the garage out of the way," he assured her. "You won't even know it's here. You're sure you don't mind?"

She shook her head.

"I know how much the car means to you and your dad. You've talked about it often enough!"

"Where's Connor?" he asked.

Their son would surely be interested in the new arrival. Connor was much the same age as William had himself been when his father had brought this car home for the first time.

Not that he'd shown he'd even been listening when the car had been discussed at his grandparents' house the other day – his headphones had remained firmly in place as he'd played on one of his games consoles.

Pam sighed.

"On the computer again. All he seems to want to do since Scott and his family moved away is play those games."

William frowned. His son had always been shy and now, with his best friend living miles away, he was spending far too much time indoors.

"The boy needs a hobby."

"He does," Pam agreed. "But persuading him isn't going to be so easy."

\* \* \* \*

Once Pam had gone back into the house, William opened the driver's side door and slipped into the car. Just sitting there reminded him of the happy

106

times spent with his father.

A sudden urge hit him. He'd love to take his family out in this car! He shook his head and patted the steering wheel. No chance of that – this poor old thing would never be roadworthy again.

"Dad?"

"In here!"

Connor appeared at the door, his eyes wide.

"Mum said you wanted to see me," he said, not taking his eyes from the car. He took a cautious few steps into the garage.

"What's this?"

William opened the passenger door for Connor to join him.

"Grandad's car."

"No, it's not. I know Grandad's car."

"This was the car he had when I was your age. It's our car now, I suppose."

"This is the one you've always gone on about?"

William smiled.

"Yep. Grandad locked it away in his garage years ago, but now that he and Gran are moving, they won't have anywhere to put it."

Connor ran a hand along the cracked dashboard.

"It's a bit of a wreck!"

"It is," William agreed sadly.

Connor was quiet for a moment as he took in the awful run-down state of the car.

"Well, what are we going to do about it?" he asked at last.

"What do you mean?" William didn't understand, though he was pleased to see his son so interested.

"It's a shame to leave it like this."

"I agree. But I don't know what we can do about it. Grandad was always going to do it up, but I'm afraid it looks as though it's too late."

"I dunno, Dad. People renovate cars all the time. I read about a man online who rebuilt an old car piece by piece, and it was in a much worse state than this one when he started!"

William considered.

"It could take ages. And it would be expensive."

"I suppose." Connor slumped back in his seat, the excited light fading from his eyes.

William was furious with himself. Connor hadn't been this animated about anything since his friend had moved away. This might well be the diversion that would lure his son away from his computer.

And if they made a mess of it, well, the car wouldn't be in a worse state than it was at the moment.

Surely it was worth a go?

"Why don't we see if we can renovate the car together?"

"Seriously, Dad? You'd let me work on it?"

Connor's eyes were shining now, and William couldn't help grinning.

"Yes, seriously." William was thoughtful for a moment as something occurred. "But it might be best if we don't say anything to Grandad just yet. I don't want to get his hopes up."

"Won't he see us working on it when he visits?"

William shook his head.

"He won't look in here."

After all, William reasoned, he'd barely looked at the car when it had sat all those years in his own garage!

Connor nodded.

"That's a good idea. It will be a nice surprise for him."

William hoped it would be.

I T took months of effort but, with the help of the internet, a manual and his neighbour, Bruce, who happened to be a mechanic, he and Connor eventually managed to get the car started.

"Sounds good," Connor said from the passenger seat as William revved the engine.

William grinned. He was beginning to think they could do this! There was still a long way to go, but now this first hurdle was over, well, it seemed as though it might be possible.

"Now we need to do something about the bodywork. There's a lot of rust. The interior could do with attention, too."

"I've been looking online," Connor said. "We can visit scrapyards, get replacements. And those things we can't find second-hand, we could have made."

The change in Connor these past few months had been remarkable. He was no longer the same boy. These days the computer was used only for homework, or to research the work they were doing on the car.

As they worked, Connor began to talk to William about new friends. Names repeatedly cropped up in conversation – people at school he'd been keeping updated about how the renovations were progressing. It seemed all the boy had needed to bring him out of himself had been a hobby.

They eventually managed to restore the car to its former glory. Bruce recommended somewhere that did a fantastic job of the paintwork. When the car was pristine and gleaming red once more, Connor invited his friends from school over to have a look at it.

"We did all the work ourselves, me and Dad!"

\* \* \* \*

"Where's Connor," Pam asked the following Sunday. "It's time he was getting ready."

### As Seen On TV

I KNOW that I know him – I've seen him before,
Not just in this movie, but loads of times more.
He starred in that drama – and also that show,
His name is – oh, darn it – just give me a mo . . .
He's always on telly – no stranger to fame,
He played in that sit-com – so what is his name?
He's been around ages, he's no passing fad,
How perfectly stupid – it's driving me mad.
But wait – yes, I've got it – oh, what a good job,
His name, I can tell you, is . . . Thingummybob!

*– Maggie Ingall.*

"Probably in the garage with the car!" William grinned. "I'll fetch him."

Sure enough, he found his son, duster in hand, polishing the red paintwork.

"My friends were asking what we're going to do with it," Connor said. "Are you going to sell it?"

William shook his head.

"I reckon we should hold on to it. You'll be sitting your driving test in a few years. We'll need another car then."

Connor's expression was disbelieving.

"You mean you're going to let me have this car?"

William smiled.

"Why not? With all the work you've put in, I reckon you've earned it. We'll have to shop around for a good deal to get you added on to the insurance. And you'll have to convince your mother that you'll be a careful driver, of course!"

Connor laughed.

"Deal!"

Pam popped her head around the garage door.

"We'll need to think about leaving in a moment. Connor, you need to go ▶

and get changed. The restaurant we're taking your grandparents to is smart."

It was another Father's Day lunch, and still his father had no idea that they'd been working on the car. They'd managed to keep it a secret this long, but today was the day to reveal all . . .

IT was with a huge sense of pride that William urged his parents outside. "What on earth . . .?" his mother started, then she saw the car. "Oh, I can't believe it!"

He glanced at his father, wondering if he'd done the right thing. Then he saw the older man's face. Silent tears were running down his face.

His father pulled out a handkerchief and blew his nose.

"I kept meaning to do the old thing up, but I could never find the parts. And as time slipped by it got into a worse and worse state. I can't believe you've done this!"

William's mother put a comforting hand on her husband's arm.

"It looks marvellous. Doesn't it, Bill?"

"It was Connor," William admitted, slapping his son on the back. "It's all down to Connor. It was his idea, and he spent hours tracking down the parts."

Connor gave a little shrug, then went to get the key from the ignition.

"Happy Father's Day, Grandad." He held out the key.

"I thought you wanted the car, Connor?" William said, perplexed.

He gave another awkward shrug.

"It will always be Grandad's car."

William's father frowned at Connor.

"I gave this car to your dad. I can't take it back, lad."

"Of course you can, Grandad," he said, waving the key before pressing it into his grandfather's hand.

His father glanced at William and William, touched by his son's generosity, nodded.

"You're named on the insurance, Dad," William told him. "Just in case you fancied going for a drive."

His dad laughed and gave in. He walked around to the driver's door.

"Well, I'm not going to say no to that! Do you fancy a spin, Connor?"

Connor grinned and headed towards the passenger side.

"Don't worry, Mum. We'll be back in time for the meal!" he called as he pulled the door closed.

"It's just like old times," William's mother said, almost to herself. Then she turned to Pam. "William and his dad used to take off in that old car at a moment's notice."

Pam smiled at William.

"I've a feeling Connor and his dad will be doing the same thing once Grandad's had his turn."

William raised his eyebrows . . . and didn't deny it. ■

110

# Windsor Castle, Windsor

**WINDSOR CASTLE** is the oldest and largest inhabited castle in the world. It has been the family home of British kings and queens for almost 1,000 years. It is an official residence of Her Majesty the Queen, whose standard flies from the Round Tower when she is in residence.

The Queen spends most of her private weekends at Windsor and takes up official residence for a month over Easter (March to April), known as Easter Court. The Queen is also at Windsor for one week each June, when she attends Royal Ascot and the service of the Order of the Garter.

Windsor is still very much a working royal palace. The castle is used regularly for ceremonial and State occasions. It is here that the Queen often hosts State Visits from overseas monarchs and presidents.

Occasionally the Queen hosts a "dine and sleep", when Her Majesty invites important figures, such as political leaders, ambassadors, high commissioners or the heads of Commonwealth nations, to have dinner at the castle before showing them a special display of items from the Royal Library. The guests then spend a night at the castle and depart after breakfast the following morning. ■

# One Good Turn

## by Linda Lewis.

WHEN I came home from the library, a letter from the supermarket was waiting for me. I scanned the all-too-familiar words.

*Reference: Trainee cashier.*

*Unfortunately, your application was not successful and the post has now been filled. Please feel free to apply again in the future.*

With a weary sigh, I put the letter away in a drawer with all the others. I'd spent almost 30 years helping my husband run his accountancy business, but when he died two years ago, the business died with him. The insurance money paid off the mortgage, but it was still a struggle. I'd been trying to find office work, but all I had managed to get so far was a part-time cleaning job at the local school. Even the local supermarket didn't want me.

It was starting to get me down. Thanks to my bicycle being out of action, I had to walk everywhere. Sometimes I found myself wishing I was older; at least then I would qualify for a free bus pass.

I switched on the TV, too tired to do very much else, but there was nothing I wanted to see, so I picked up the crossword instead.

I had only managed one clue when the doorbell rang.

A forlorn-looking man stood on the doorstep, clutching a glossy brochure. In his fifties, he had greying hair and nice eyes, though at the moment they looked anxious. He put on a smile and beamed at me.

"Hello, can I interest you in this wonderful catalogue? It's called 'All Our Yesterdays' and it's packed full –"

"No, thanks," I interrupted. "I'm a bit short of money right now. Besides, I've seen those before. There's nothing I really need."

The man's shoulders slumped as though all the air had been sucked out of him.

"This is hopeless," he said. "I'm not getting anywhere. You're the first person in two hours who's actually bothered to answer the door."

"Stop right there," I said firmly. "I'm not interested in your tales of woe. I've got my own problems."

To my surprise, the man sighed.

"I was a silly old fool to take his job. I'm not a salesperson. All I can do is fix things." He straightened his shoulders and looked me in the eye. "I'm very sorry to have disturbed you. Good day." With that, he turned and started to walk away.

I'm not sure why I did it, but I stopped him. I think it was because I recognised something in him – pride, a spark of determination – that

Illustration by Mandy Dixon/Thinkstockphotos.

reminded me of my own problems finding suitable employment. He'd also given me an idea.

"Wait just a moment. You said you can fix things. Could you do anything with an old bicycle? The lights won't work and it needs a puncture mended. I couldn't pay very much, mind."

Immediately the man's eyes brightened.

"I'm not sure, but I might as well have a look at it while I'm here." He held out his hand. "My name's Jim. Jim Thomson."

"Shelagh Marks." We shook hands very formally, then I led him out to the garden where my bicycle stood propped up against the wall. I hadn't been able to use it since the tyre had gone flat.

The man inspected it and after a minute or so he nodded.

113

## A Tranquil Wood

TO walk within a tranquil wood
On a day that's bright and fair,
Delights us with the lovely things,
That nature gives us there.

Pale primroses beside our path,
New tender leaves above,
A bluebell sea spread far and wide,
A picture that we love.

A cool escape from summer's heat,
A calm and leafy bower,
Where woodland creatures take their rest,
Until the twilight hour.

"The dynamo's broken."

"Is that something you could fix?"

"I should think so," he said. "The trouble is, I don't have my tools with me."

"No problem," I said. "There are loads in the shed." I flung open the door. "Help yourself."

"Wow!" Jim cried as he looked at the neatly arranged shelves, each one crammed with tools and other hardware.

I laughed. He looked like a little boy faced with a pile of presents on Christmas morning.

"They belonged to my late husband. As you can see, he loved DIY," I told him.

JIM had already taken the bicycle into the shed and was sifting through a large box of assorted spanners.

"It shouldn't take me very long," he said, as he flipped the bike upside-down. I could see that he knew what he was doing.

"I hate to ask, but before you do anything, do you have any idea how much it will cost?" I asked.

"A fiver should cover it."

"Really?" I was shocked. "That's great. While you're busy, why don't I take your catalogue to my friend's house?"

"Thanks, but I'll be very surprised if you get anywhere. People just don't have the money for luxuries right now," he said as he started to

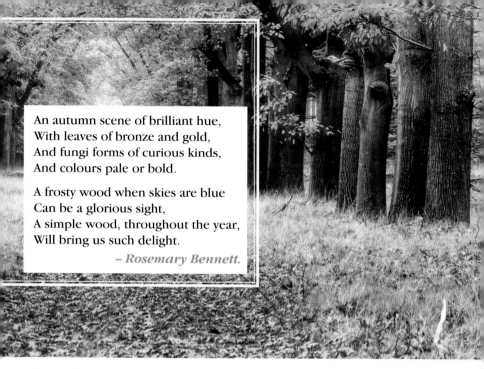

An autumn scene of brilliant hue,
With leaves of bronze and gold,
And fungi forms of curious kinds,
And colours pale or bold.

A frosty wood when skies are blue
Can be a glorious sight,
A simple wood, throughout the year,
Will bring us such delight.

*— Rosemary Bennett.*

dismantle the dynamo.

"Maybe so, but let me give it a go. I've always enjoyed selling."

I left him to it. Forty-five minutes later, I was back. I headed out to the shed where Jim was waiting for me.

"All done," he said, proudly patting the saddle of the bike.

"Thank you ever so much. This is for you." I handed him a large order.

He took one look and gasped.

"How did you manage that? This is more than I've sold in a month!"

"I used to be in sales years ago, before I got married. I'd love a job like yours, but so far I haven't been able to convince anyone to give me a chance." I told him all about it. "Over the past year, I've applied for literally dozens of jobs. Most of the time, I don't even get an interview. Employers aren't interested in a fifty-four-year-old woman with no references. I spent the last twenty-odd years working from home for my husband."

"They don't know what they're missing." Jim was still gazing at the order form I'd given him. "I'd never have been able to land an order as big as this."

I went over to the bike.

"And I could never do something like this. It looks as good as new. You've even polished the saddle."

He started telling me what he'd done to mend the dynamo, but I raised a hand to stop him.

"You're wasting your time. My husband used to say that when it came to anything mechanical, he would have been better off explaining it to a

**115**

hedgehog. He was right, too." I laughed.

"That wasn't very kind." He sighed forlornly. "It's a shame you can't take over my job. I'm on a two-month trial. If I don't start selling soon, they won't keep me on."

I took a five-pound note from my bag and offered it to him, but he waved it away.

"Thanks, but I can't take that. Not when you've got me that amazing order."

"Thanks." As I put the money back in my purse, I had another thought. "I was wondering – have you ever considered starting up as an odd-job man?"

"Yes, only I'd never be able to cope. I'm completely useless when it comes to paperwork. This is bad enough." He waved the catalogue.

I smiled.

"Fancy a cup of tea? I have an idea. Maybe we can help each other."

OVER two cups of tea and half a packet of chocolate digestives, I outlined my plan. If he spoke to his boss to see if I could take over his sales round, I would help him start up as a self-employed odd job man, doing his accounts and paperwork for a small fee.

Luckily, he was as excited by the idea as I was.

It worked like a charm. As soon as Jim's boss saw the order, they were delighted to let me take over his round.

Soon I was earning enough money to buy the things I needed. I was even managing to put a few pounds a week away towards a holiday.

It wasn't long before Jim's business took off, too. It seemed there wasn't much he couldn't fix.

"He's amazing," my best friend, Hazel, gushed one afternoon. "He came round to mend my lawnmower and stayed to fix that dripping tap. I was so delighted, I asked him out to dinner, but he turned me down flat. He said there was somebody else. I thought he was single?"

I laughed. That was typical of Hazel. She never wastes any time. If she's interested in a man, she just comes out with it. Me, I wouldn't know where to start.

"He is. He lost his wife three years ago. Maybe you're not his type and he was letting you down gently."

"Or," she said with just a hint of a smile, "he's been seeing somebody and hasn't told you about it."

For some reason, that thought niggled away in my mind. If Jim was seeing somebody, I didn't understand why he hadn't mentioned it to me. In the weeks we'd been working together, I'd come to think of Jim as a good friend. Maybe we weren't as close as I had thought.

What bothered me was why I was so upset about it. I started to think it might be better if we parted company. Now his business was set up and everything was running smoothly, he didn't really need me any more, anyway.

I called him that evening.

"It's my birthday on Friday. Let's go out to dinner for a farewell meal," I suggested.

"What do you mean by a farewell meal?" he asked, sounding confused.

"I meant you can manage the paperwork on your own now the systems have been set up. You don't need my help any more," I explained.

"True, but I'm only coping with any of it because you've made it all so simple."

He wasn't making this easy.

"I'm glad to have helped, but we agreed this was only meant to be a temporary arrangement. I'll book a table at Figaro's for eight o'clock," I told him.

This time he didn't argue.

"All right, but I'm paying."

THE night of my birthday, I had terrible trouble deciding what to wear. As I tried on yet another outfit, I wondered what was wrong with me. It was as I checked my appearance in the full-length mirror for the umpteenth time that I realised the truth. It wasn't having a job or enough money that was making me feel so much happier – it was Jim. I was going to miss him more than I could say.

The restaurant was wonderful, and the food and the wine were, too, but all I kept thinking was what if this is the last time I ever see Jim?

While we were waiting for our desserts to arrive, I asked him about Hazel.

"Hazel tells me she asked you out to dinner and you turned her down flat." I picked up the bottle of wine and began topping up our glasses.

He nodded.

"That's right. I told her I wasn't interested. There's only room for one woman in my life. Her name's Shelagh Marks."

As he said my name, I was so shocked I almost knocked his glass over.

Jim sighed.

"So, now you know. I've wanted to tell you how I felt for ages, but you kept saying you didn't want another man in your life. Now we're parting company, I don't need to hide how I feel any more." He looked into my eyes, making my heart do a backwards somersault. "Happy birthday, Shelagh. Thanks for making these past few months so wonderful." He raised his glass. "To you."

I reached out and put my hand over his.

"You'd better make that 'To us'!"

For a few seconds which felt like an eternity, there was silence.

"Do you mean that?" he asked eventually.

"Yes. I love you, Jim."

"And I love you." Then he grinned and called out to the waiter. "Can we have some champagne, please? We're celebrating!" ▮

DIANA FOR GIRLS 1965

## Diana 1965

THE first "Diana" annual, published in 1965, was proud to proclaim that it was for "girls who are keen on fashion, ballet, nursing, ponies, dramatics, history, wild life, dancing, sport" and the book gave those first readers all those and more!

In the year when Mary Quant made the miniskirt the height of fashion, "Diana" girls were learning about the top designers Coco Chanel, Simonetta, Clodagh and Mary Quant in the pages of their annual. Maureen, the "Hollywood Reporter", spilled the beans on what young film stars Kym Karath, Angela Cartwright, Marta Kristen and Ralph Hart were getting up to in "Starlet Corner".

Dancing queens were kept happy with plenty of articles and stories featuring all styles from Chinese ballet to the Twist, and pony fans were in for a real treat with 10 whole pages of pony fun and games. Picture stories and longer reads completed the picture, giving the Sixties Miss plenty to keep her busy after unwrapping her Christmas annual. ■

*Illustration by Mark Viney.*

# Making Ends Meet

## by Christine Evans.

THE thing I dreaded about retirement was the sudden drop in our income. So Jack, my husband, and I sat down to have another look at our budget.

"I often wonder how our parents managed, Sandra," Jack said.

"Make do and mend," I told him with a smile. "My mother could make a meal out of nothing for the six of us."

"Mine, too," my husband replied with a fond smile. "I was having a nosy at your magazine the other day and I noticed an ad for an old-fashioned cookbook. I recognised half the recipes mentioned as ones Ma made. I could almost taste that rabbit stew and dumplings. Oh, and shepherd's pie, too. How come you never make that any more, Sandra?"

"I never had time when I came home from work," I said. "I've more time now I've retired so maybe I'll make one soon."

"Perhaps we should send for one of those cookbooks," my husband suggested.

"No need," I told him. "I've still got my mother's cookbook somewhere. I'll dig it out."

That afternoon I hauled myself up into the loft and began rummaging in an old cardboard suitcase full of memorabilia. If it hadn't been so cold up there I could have spent all afternoon reliving my past.

I found Mother's cookbook. It wasn't a proper printed book, just an old exercise book that she'd begun with school lessons and then added to when she'd married. It was backed with brown paper and all the original times and temperatures, written for use with a black-leaded range, had been altered in a different pen once she'd used a gas cooker.

Luckily, I only had brothers, otherwise the book might not have ended up with me. I had an electric cooker, so I'd have to work out the settings afresh. Tucking my precious book under my arm, I renegotiated the loft ladder.

THE old recipe book was tatty and covered in food stains. The pages felt very fragile as I tentatively turned them and saw all the old favourites my mother had made for her growing family. In the back was tucked an old shopping list. I chuckled when I read it. Among her list of essentials there was flour and lard for all her pies and suet for the dumplings and pastry. There were lentils and pearl barley to bulk up her stews. The mixed fruit jam on the list was cheaper than strawberry, which we rarely had.

At the bottom of the list was the inevitable pound of broken biscuits. I can still see those deep square tins lined up in the grocer's. They had glass windows inset into the lids so that we could see the biscuits inside. I loved to see the little red hearts of the jammy dodgers peeping out of their tin, but unfortunately they always seemed too robust to get broken. The tin at the end held all the biscuits that had been damaged and chipped.

I never got to the custard creams before my brothers, and Dad always had to have the gingers because he was the breadwinner. I can see my brother, Ricky, on the back step, licking the custard cream filling off the split biscuit.

He wouldn't have dared do it in front of Mother. Woe betide any of us who dunked, too, as it was seen as the height of bad manners by my parents. We may have been poor but my parents insisted on standards.

I remember Aunt Avis, my mother's sister. She was the one with pretensions, as she'd married a Naval officer. Mother always kept two china cups and saucers for when my aunt arrived for a cup of tea. The china was the last remnant of my grandmother's precious tea set. When my aunt paid us a

120

visit I offered her a plate holding some biscuits.

"Have a nice biscuit, Auntie," I offered politely, hoping she'd leave the custard creams.

"They call them 'Nice', dear. It's a place in France," she said, correcting my pronunciation.

I thought they were nice whichever way you pronounced it, and I continued to pronounce it my way, despite my aunt. She had chocolate fingers at her house, and Garibaldis. She was the one who brought my mother a box of Scottish shortbread back from a holiday in Dunoon. The first time I tasted real shortbread I was hooked. How could those soft, buttery, melt-in-the mouth biscuits have the same name as the hard, tasteless things that were usually all that was left in the bottom of our barrel of broken biscuits?

ARMED with my cookbook, I went into the kitchen to decide what to make first. Steak and kidney pudding looked good and filling, so I put suet on my shopping list and set off for the supermarket. I searched the meat aisles in vain.

"We don't sell kidney," the helpful man in the company sweatshirt said. "An independent butcher might."

I made my other purchases and loaded them into the car then headed for the high street. I found the butcher's and stood in the queue. Trade was busy and people were chatting about how they'd decided to forsake the supermarket meat counters in favour of the local butcher.

'Suits me!" the smiling butcher in the striped apron said. "At least you know what you're getting in our shop."

"Do you sell lamb's kidney?" I asked when it was my turn.

"Certainly do, madam," he said. "How much?"

I'd spotted a recipe for devilled kidneys in the book so I bought enough for that, too.

"I don't buy offal," the woman behind me in the queue said, reminding me instantly of Aunt Avis.

"It's very good for you," the butcher replied cheerfully. "You won't get anaemic eating my offal."

I glanced round his counter and remembered the shepherd's pie recipe.

"I'll have a pound of mince, too," I said.

"I never buy mince," the lady said. "My husband says you don't know what's in it."

"There's only the best steak goes into my mince," the butcher said with a frown.

His sausages looked delicious, plump and juicy. I knew Jack's cholesterol was a bit dodgy, but he loved sausages and mash, so I decided to buy some and bake them to release most of the fat.

"And some sausages," I said.

## Crunch Time

WHAT could be more satisfactory?
What more pleasing place to be –
Here, within a dappled orchard,
Picking apples from a tree.
Russets bronze, and Pippins rosy,
All profusion, crisp and sweet,
Now at last, as each fruit ripens,
Now we gather nature's treat.
Fill your bags and fill your baskets,
Autumn gives us gifts galore,
Some for pies and some for crumbles,
Some to eat and some to store.
Here, beneath the spreading branches,
Who on earth would not agree
This is just the perfect pastime,
Picking apples from a tree.

*– Maggie Ingall.*

The woman beside me nearly had palpitations.

"Oh, I never buy sausages," she declared. "You never –"

The butcher interrupted.

"There's only the best ingredients go into my sausages. Mark, serve this lady, will you?" he directed his young assistant, who'd just arrived with a tray of newly cut lamb chops.

"I'll have two small cutlets," she said with a sniff.

The butcher glared after her as the woman left with her purchase and muttered under his breath.

There were lots of cuts of meat in his counter that my mother had once used. He had neck-end chops and breast of lamb – things I hadn't spotted in the supermarket. I bought some skirt of beef for my pudding. He broke into smiles as he totted up my order.

"Hope everything is to your satisfaction, madam," he said with a grin.

"I'm sure it will be," I told him, smiling back. I hadn't been called madam for ages.

On the way back to the car I passed a wholefood shop and nipped in for some lentils and barley. I also bought some apricots to make Jack's favourite Moroccan lamb stew. I chuckled as I could almost hear my father's voice . . .

"Apricots are fruit! You can't put fruit in stew!"
Oh, how tastes change!

BACK home I rolled out my suet pastry and lined a pot then loaded it with steak, kidney and gravy. It seemed to take ages on the cooker and I wondered if it was actually as economical as I'd hoped. Somewhere in the back of my cupboard I had a pressure cooker which would save electricity if I used it. It needed a few new parts so I resolved to call at the hardware shop on the high street and see if they had the bits in stock.

I'd been very pleased with my trip that morning and I decided to use my bus pass to go shopping on the high street in the future. I hadn't had time to shop about when I was working, and the car park was always packed on Saturdays.

✳    ✳    ✳    ✳

The pudding was a great success. Jack sighed in contentment and patted his stomach.

"That was lovely! Just like Ma used to make it," he said.

But an hour later he was asking for the antacid tablets.

▶

"I think that suet pastry is a bit heavy for me these days," he confessed. All week I used my mother's cookbook, but by the end of the week we felt bloated.

"I think those recipes were meant for men doing heavy manual work and lively growing kids," Jack decided. "When I come to think of it, Ma ate very little herself, though she piled up Dad's plate."

We'd just had cheese and onion pie that Friday, and to be honest my arthritis wasn't responding well to all the pastry.

I thought back on the past. As we children became older and there was more demand on the family budget, Mother had decided that she might get a job. Aunt Avis recommended her for work at a catalogue firm and, although Dad wasn't keen, she really enjoyed it.

Soon our diet changed, and there was more convenience food on the table. Mother was tired after a full day's work and at weekends we all had to help with the cleaning. But she did a very tasty version of shepherd's pie with a couple of tins of stewed steak and some mashed potato on top. On Fridays we were treated to fish and chips from the chip shop. Eventually her cookbook was relegated to the back of the kitchen drawer and finally ended up in my loft. I'd resorted to convenience food many times myself while I was working, but now I was at leisure to try different recipes and to shop around.

I SOON had a tasty repertoire of home-made soups, and my slow cooker was being used more – a luxury my mother never had while she was working. The pressure cooker was handy, too, so I hoped my fuel bills would fall despite all this slow-cooking.

"Perhaps we'll have some salads next week, or a vegetarian dish," I suggested.

"Vegetarian?" Jack was as apoplectic as the woman in the butcher's.

But sticking to the economy drive, I stewed the remains of the joint from Sunday on Monday, just as Mother had. Then on Tuesday I made a vegetable lasagne, and Jack didn't notice there was no meat in it.

"I love Italian food," he said, smiling. "We never had it as nippers. How about a nice curry some time?"

It seemed that our mothers' way of cooking wasn't the only way to save money. I resolved to nip into the library when I was next on the high street and find some different recipes now I had more time on my hands. Also, our new budget had left something to spare for a holiday.

"There's a coach tour to Dunoon here," Jack said, glancing up from the local evening newspaper. "It's quite reasonable. We can book any time we like, now we're not working. Do you fancy it?"

Dunoon? I thought instantly of that first taste of real shortbread.

"I certainly do." ▪

## *Malham, Yorkshire*

MALHAM is a small village in the Pennines, at the southern base of the Yorkshire Dales. It's a pretty place, surrounded by limestone dry-stone walls and with a stream running right through the middle of the village.

Mentioned in the Domesday book as "Malgun", Malham has been a settlement for at least 1,000 years. Traces of Iron Age boundaries are still visible today. Nowadays, hill farms and tourism are the main activities but 100 years ago Malham was a place of mills and mines.

From Malham itself, an easy walk of 800 metres takes you to magnificent Malham Cove. Climb the rock stones on the left and you will reach the top of the cove and have one of most impressive views of the whole Yorkshire Dales. Underfoot is the limestone pavement created by a waterfall about 50,000 years ago, and in front is a magnificent view of Airedale.

You can see Malham Cove and its famous limestone pavement in "Harry Potter And The Deathly Hallows – Part 1". ■

# Free Falling

## by Angela Lanyon.

S O you won't mind, will you?"

"Of course not, Robin, that'll be lovely."

I put the phone down in the cradle and leaned back in the chair. Oh, dear.

I supposed it would be all right. But it was nearly 18 months since I had seen my granddaughter, and in that time I knew she'd have changed.

What a roller-coaster of a time it had been! I'd had a knee replacement, and Alice had finished her finals and got a first-class degree in maths. Since then she'd been around the world and now had landed a job with a prestigious firm in London.

And me? Well, I fall apart at the mere thought of maths! I can manage my money – since I've been on my own I've had to. But anything else? Well, I don't think I feel much different about sums from those days when I'd take one look at my algebra homework and burst into tears!

✳    ✳    ✳    ✳

"How long is she staying?" Betty, my neighbour, asked me when I popped round for a cuppa and told her all about it. "Only overnight? Well, that's nothing to worry about."

"I don't know." I shook my head and patted my stick, which was leaning against the side of the sofa. "She'll think I'm a real old crock."

"Well, you are, aren't you, Marge?" She pushed a plate of gingernuts towards me. "Thinking of getting Botox?"

"Not at all!" I said indignantly. "All the same . . ."

When we'd been younger, Alice and I, we'd walked for miles. A good tramp, we used to call it, to get rid of the cobwebs. But now? Well, I could get to the shops, no bother, and was back to driving my little Mini. Truth be told, however, I was feeling quite a different person from how I'd been before my knee had been fixed, even if I didn't admit it.

Nevertheless, that was no reason for Betty calling me an old crock. Old crock yourself, I thought!

"Don't worry, it'll be all right." Betty was refilling my cup. "You'll just have to think of something to do with her. After all, she'll not be here all that long. And you know youngsters – part of the time she'll be in her bed!"

That was true, I reflected as I got my supper and settled myself down for a nice evening of telly.

"Winter drawers on!" I muttered to myself with a giggle as I pulled the curtains shut. Not that it was really cold yet, but I was certainly glad of the

gas fire and my cosy home.

I'd loved the autumn when I'd been younger, kicking my way through the dead leaves.

"They sound just like my breakfast does, Nana!" Alice had said, jumping down from a tree stump into a big pile of crunchy, bronze beech leaves, before picking up an armful and showering them all over me.

She'd be too old for that sort of thing now.

I took down the last photo Robin had sent to me when Alice had been in Australia. Oz, her dad called it. There she was, free-fall parachuting! Enough to take your breath away, although it was something maybe I would have tried when I'd been younger. If they'd had such things back then. I could see so much of myself in Alice, from her dark shining hair which fell in a sheepdog fringe over her face, to her love of adventure. Just because you get old, it doesn't mean you don't fancy trying out new things.

And there was her picture on the wall facing me, in the cap and gown when she'd got her degree. What a happy day that was. I'd had the photo framed, though Robin had insisted on paying for it.

"She is my daughter, you know, Mum, as well as your granddaughter!"

Alice looked so smart when I saw her last. I was staying with them over the Easter weekend and she'd been going off out with her latest boyfriend. Elegant wasn't the word! Legs that seemed to start somewhere about her armpits, and wearing black shiny tights with a flouncy emerald skirt and scoop-necked top. You could tell how proud her mum and dad were just by looking at their faces.

That had been nearly 18 months ago.

A COUPLE of weeks later found me making up the spare bed for Alice's arrival.

"First the foot and then the head, that's the way to make a bed," I used to tell her long ago, as we smoothed down the under sheet and tucked in the blankets.

That was when we had blankets, instead of cosy duvets you could wrap around you.

Now I was shaking out a nice flowery cover that smelled of fresh air and the lavender bags that I'd made and put in the airing cupboard with the big fluffy towels. I bet she'd not had those when she'd been backpacking round Asia!

How she'd loved snuggling down when she stayed with me. When it was winter I wrapped the eiderdown around her and then I sat on the bed, with her leaning against me. I drew back the curtains so we could look at the stars.

"There's Orion," I said, pointing at the big square of shining stars. "Can you see the dog running after him?"

"The stars are millions of light years away, Nana," she told me, fascinated

## Small Adventures

HAVE a small adventure when you can,
Nothing too outrageous or extreme,
Switching off from every mundane task,
Just escaping, following a dream.
Strolling on a pathway in the sun,
Going somewhere you have never been,
Searching for a book to give you pleasure,
Watching cheerful films you've never
    seen.

Give yourself a little treat sometimes,
Tea and cakes, or sweets, or something
    new,
Special treats can help to lift the spirit,
Reminding you that you are special, too.
With old friends enjoy the reminiscing,
Meet new people, they have things to
    say,
Look around, there's so much to
    discover,
Have a small adventure every day!

– *Iris Hesselden.*

by numbers even when she was little.

She never tired of telling me how fast light moved, and how long it would take you to get to the moon. Some nights my head would be spinning by the time I switched the lights off and left her to settle down to sleep. I'm sure she dreamed in numbers!

\* \* \* \*

My knee was still giving me gyp if I was on my feet for too long. Having made the bed, I slumped down on it – only for a moment, mind – and stared out at the sky. It was late summer now. I wondered if she'd see Orion, even when it got dark.

She would still recognise Willow Cottage across the road, though. Would she remember the time she got lost? What a day that was! One minute she was playing in the garden, digging in a flower-bed, and the next minute there wasn't a sign of her.

My heart was in my mouth. Where had she gone? What could I possibly

129

say to Robin and Jill if anything had happened to her?

I needn't have worried, as it turned out. Adventurous from the word go, Alice had decided to see what was across the road. Aged three. I ask you!

Colin Wilson brought her back to me.

"This your granddaughter? She was looking for buried treasure in my garden." He laughed.

I didn't know whether to smack or hug her as she stood there, grinning all over her face and waving her little red plastic spade. What I did was pick her up and squeeze her tight, because I could see the expression on my face had upset her and she was going to cry.

"Be a good girl in future and stay in Nana's garden," I told her when we got back inside.

Well, she'd certainly done a lot more than cross the road over the years.

I WAS halfway down the stairs when a sudden thought struck me. When you've been all round the world, do you really want to come and visit your old nana? A cold feeling crept round my heart as I remembered it hadn't been Alice who'd asked if she could come and stay. It had been her dad. Robin had always been one for doing the right thing, and had no doubt suggested it to her.

So maybe she didn't want to come at all. Maybe this was no more than a duty visit . . .

I asked Betty what she thought. We were sitting outside in the garden, each of us with a mug of coffee.

"I think you're making a mountain out of a mole hill. How old is Alice? Twenty-two?"

I nodded.

"In that case, you're fine. She wouldn't come if she didn't want to. Kids that age don't."

"Alice isn't a kid. It's not like she was still in her teens."

"Take my word for it." Betty had seven grandchildren. "She'll know fine what she wants, and you might as well save your breath to cool your porridge. If she wants to see you, she'll come. If she doesn't, wild horses wouldn't drag her!"

\* \* \* \*

I thought about that as I went round the supermarket on the morning she was due to arrive. I was looking for things I thought she might like and seeing how far the money would stretch. Alice had always liked my cooking, though the nearest I could get her to making something herself had been licking out the bowl when I'd been baking.

When I got home I set the table in the window of my lounge diner and put out a nice salad, topped with parsley out of the garden, and

130

some ham that I'd boiled.

I looked around. Everything was ready . . . except me. I was still wearing my apron and my hair was all sticking out, and here was Alice, coming up the path with a big grin on her face,

When I opened the door she gave me a hug that almost cracked my ribs.

"I'm all messy!" I protested, pulling back to look at her.

She hadn't changed, not much. She was still willowy and her blue eyes still sparkled, but she looked so grown-up. And tanned!

"You look lovely," I said. "Turn round and let me look at you."

She did so and then pulled a bottle of wine from her bag. When I told her I thought it was bit early for me to be drinking she laughed and said it was to celebrate her new job!

"One glass with lunch, Nana, and we'll save the rest for tonight," she coaxed.

Well, after that, I couldn't refuse.

"And while we're having lunch you'll have to tell me all about it. And all about your travels."

It seemed she'd been everywhere – Thailand, New Zealand, Mexico. And the things she'd done! My heart sank. Whatever were we going to do to compete with all that?

"What would you like to do this afternoon?"

"Cooking."

I nearly fell off my chair.

"Cooking?" I repeated.

"The thing is, Nana, I'm getting this flat, and I'll have to cook for myself. I don't want to rely on packet foods and bought stuff all the time!"

IT was a good job, I decided as I watched Alice write down the recipes later that afternoon, that I had a well-stocked store cupboard. We'd made meatballs in my own special, spicy tomato sauce, and a lemon meringue pie, and now we were finishing off the bottle of wine.

"Nana, you know my flat I've told you about?"

I nodded.

"I don't suppose, that is, I just wondered . . . You see, now you've got your new knee, I wondered if you'd come to London on the train, and I could show it to you. Maybe stay for a weekend? I'd love to take you around."

Me, go to London? Whatever was Alice thinking?

But then I had a thought. Going to London certainly wasn't as risky as free-fall parachuting, after all.

"That's a great idea," I said. "What's more, I'll treat us to one of those big musicals. I've always wanted to see 'Phantom'!"

Two months later I proudly showed Betty the souvenir programme.

"Who's the old crock now?" I asked her. ■

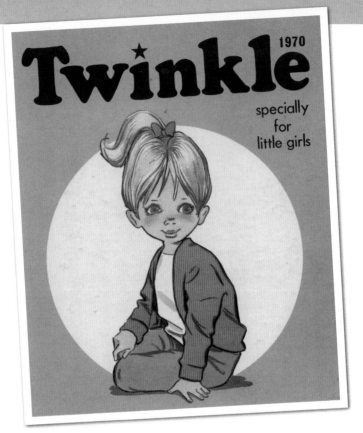

1970

# Twinkle

specially
for
little girls

## ———— Twinkle 1970 ————

IN the year we said goodbye to the half-crown piece, the ten-shilling note and the Beatles, little girls said hello to the very first Twinkle annual. Characters familiar from the weekly comic, which began in January 1968, were to be found in its pages. "The Three Pennys", about three little girls called Penny Smith, Penny Henry and Penny Wilson, "Sally Sweet Of Sunshine Street" and Twinkle herself appeared in fresh, new stories alongside lots of ideas for fun things to make and do. Like Dana's Eurovision-winning song that year, "Twinkle" treated its readers to "All Kinds Of Everything"!

While the characters in their older sisters' comics featured heroines who were real nurses and animal trainers, "Twinkle" encouraged its little readers with stories about "Nurse Nancy" the young granddaughter of the man who ran the local doll's hospital and "Sue Of The Children's Zoo", whose parents allowed her to help to look after the animals in the zoo they owned. And, of course, no book for little girls would have been complete without cute pictures of kittens – no doubt extra popular in the year that Walt Disney's "The Aristocats" was released in the cinema! ■

*Illustration by Jim Dewar/Thinkstockphotos.*

# A Box Of Memories

## by Katie Payne.

BOX?" My daughter Ruth looked quizzically at Amy, my granddaughter. "What for?"

"For school," Amy replied, staring at the television. "Mrs Greene wants us to make a memory box." She shuffled down further in her chair. "Although I don't see the point, really."

I put down the magazine I'd been reading.

"Don't you have any memories you'd like to keep, Amy?"

"Dunno." Amy flicked a glance to me, then away again.

"Well, I think it sounds like a great idea," I said. "I'm sure you'd have plenty of things to put in one."

"Maybe," Amy replied.

"I've got a memory box, you know," I said.

▶

133

"Really?" Amy finally tore her eyes away from the television and looked at me properly.

"I've had it for over sixty years," I said, pleased that I could sense a flicker of interest in Amy's eyes. "We did one at school, too. When I was about your age, actually."

"And you've kept it all these years?" Amy asked incredulously.

"Of course!" I laughed. "Isn't that the point? To keep your precious memories close to you for ever?"

"That box has gone with Grandma wherever she's been." Ruth came and sat on the edge of the sofa, smiling. "Through her marriage to Grandad, to when your uncle David and I were born, right through to when you and Lucy came along."

"Where is it now?" Amy asked.

"In my room upstairs," I replied. "It came with me when I moved in with you all."

I thought for a moment.

"I still take it out and look through it sometimes," I said. "If I'm feeling a bit sad, I can look at what's in there. It brings back so many happy memories, it's hard to be sad for too long."

"Do you know," Ruth said, "it's been a while since we had a look through it, hasn't it?"

"Could we?" Amy sat up straighter and leaned over to me.

"Would you be interested?" I asked.

"I'd love to see it, Grandma!" Amy grinned.

"Well then, I'll fetch it down right now!" I said.

It was true; the box had remained unopened for some time. Perhaps this was the ideal opportunity to have another trip down memory lane.

"I have a suggestion," Ruth said, getting up and finding a pen and notepad. "While Grandma shows you what's in her box, why don't you make a list of what you'd like to go into yours?"

She handed Amy the pen and notepad.

"It might give you some good ideas."

My box was where it always was, at the back of my wardrobe, slotted in between shoes and handbags that I'd long since worn or used. I picked it up, wiping a thin layer of dust from it, and carried it downstairs.

It was a plain brown shoebox, with *Lilley and Skinner* printed ornately across the lid. I felt the familiar ripple of anticipation as I thought about what was inside.

"I started this in nineteen forty-eight," I told Amy, lifting the lid and putting it carefully to one side.

"I can't believe you've kept it all this time!" She peered into it. "It's like a museum in a box!" She put her fingers in and gently sifted through the contents.

134

Then she looked up.

"Do you still have the shoes from this box?" she asked hopefully.

"No, they've long since gone." I laughed. "I'd never get my feet into them now, anyway!"

"Were they dancing shoes?" Amy asked. "Mum says you danced a lot when you were younger."

"Sadly, no. But there weren't so many dancing shoes in the Forties. Don't forget we'd just had a war."

I thought for a moment.

"All those fancy shoes we'd had in the Thirties disappeared once the war started, you see?" I said. "We had to be practical."

"You were taught to look after your things, too," Ruth said knowingly.

"We were. There was no such thing as throwing something out if it broke and buying a new one."

"Which reminds me," Ruth said, looking at Amy. "We need to talk about those new shoes of yours that you've already managed to scuff!"

"We used to repair our shoes," I said, smiling. "Your great-grandad used to mend all ours at home . . ."

My voice trailed off as I remembered seeing my father marching down to the shed at the end of our garden, a handful of shoes with him. Sometimes I'd go with him, watching spellbound as he'd expertly tap away at the soles with a small hammer, before bringing them back to my mother.

His words and voice still sat in my memory.

"That'll be good for a good few months now, Sylvia," he'd say, pleased as Punch with his handiwork.

"What's this?" Amy's voice roused me from my memories as she pulled out a rolled-up magazine, carefully secured with a rubber band.

I took it from her, unfurled it and spread it out on my lap.

"Ah, this was a magazine called 'Film Reel' that I used to like reading," I said, smiling. "And I kept this one particularly because it had my favourite actress in it." I tapped the grainy black and white photo of Jean Simmons on the front cover.

"Did you read it a lot?" Amy asked, gazing at the picture.

I nodded.

"It was my treat. Mother would give me a shilling and the man who ran the corner shop always kept a copy for me. Once I had read it, it was agony having to wait for the next issue!" I told her. "It used to take for ever – or so I thought at the time."

"I can't imagine that," Amy said, frowning.

"So, what magazine would you put in your box today, Amy?" Ruth asked.

Amy shrugged.

"I don't really read them, do I?" she said. "Everything I need to know is on the internet, so I guess I'll just download and print a picture of my favourite actor, and put that in instead."

She wrote something down on her notepad.

"There was nothing quite like opening those brand-new pages and seeing what delights were waiting for me inside," I said, rolling the magazine up and placing it back in the shoebox. "Not quite the same, downloading and printing, is it?"

I looked into my box again.

"And, of course, you know who these people are," I said, carefully picking up a photo. "That's you, in the dress, and that's Great-grandad and Great-grandma."

Amy pointed to my parents.

"Mum's shown me pictures of them before." She stared hard at the photo. "But I don't know who that man is in the uniform." She glanced up at me. "It's not Grandad, is it?"

"No," I said, tracing my finger across the photo. "This is my older brother, Frank. Your great-uncle."

"I never knew him, did I?"

I gazed fondly down at Frank's young, fresh face.

"No, you didn't," I replied. "He died not long after this photo was taken."

"So why is he in uniform?" Amy asked, peering at Frank. "He looked very smart in it, didn't he?"

"He did," I replied.

I remembered the day, only a few weeks after the photo had been taken, when my father received the telegram, telling us the news that Frank had been killed in action.

"He was nineteen when this photo was taken. It was nineteen forty-three, and Frank was home on leave from France for a few days."

"And you've kept his photo all this time?" Amy asked. "That's awesome!"

I glanced at my daughter and caught her eye, smiling.

"I have lots of photos of Frank," I said. "But this is my favourite because it's the only one I have of us all together. I like to get it out and look at it now and then, just to remember my brother and to let him know I'm still thinking of him."

"I'll definitely put a photo of my family in my box, too, then," Amy said firmly. "Of you, Grandma; and of me and Mum, Dad and Lucy, of course."

She took the photo from me and looked at it.

"Then, whenever I get my memory box out, I can look at it and think about the day I went through your box with you." Amy smiled. "It'll help me to remember you, just like your photo helps you to remember your brother."

"I think that's a wonderful idea," I said, patting her arm affectionately.

"What's this?" Amy pulled a small scrap of material from the box.

'Oh, goodness me! This is a piece of chiffon from my very first dance dress." I laughed. "My parents bought it for me as a treat so I could wear it to a Christmas ball. They saved up for six months to buy it for me!"

I thought back to the day I'd been given the dress, and recalled the feeling of utter joy at opening the department store's box and seeing my new dress inside. It had been wrapped in tissue paper, I remembered. Carefully opening the tissue to reveal my beautiful turquoise dress had been the most wonderful feeling.

"Six months?" Amy laughed. "I don't believe you!"

"Truly," I said, nodding. "They bought it for me when I was nineteen, so that must have been in, let me see . . . nineteen fifty-two."

"If I want something, Dad just puts it on his credit card and pays for it later," Amy said, confused. "Why didn't your parents do that to buy you your dress?"

"Ordinary folk didn't have credit cards back then," I said, amused at her puzzled face. "If you wanted something, you saved up until you could afford it. Simple as that."

I held the turquoise chiffon gently in my hands.

"When the dress didn't fit me any more, I couldn't bear the thought of never seeing it again." I sighed. "I snipped a small piece from it and put it into my memory box, so that I could look at it again and remind myself that, yes, I really did used to wear dresses like this!"

Amy stared at my box, her brow creased.

"I think, perhaps," she finally said slowly, "sometimes I take the things that I have in life for granted."

"In what way?" her mother urged.

"Just that, I can have everything I want, whenever I want it," Amy replied. She put the end of her pen in her mouth and chewed it, lost in thought.

"If I want to find out about something, I use the internet," she went on at last. "If I want a new pair of shoes because I'm bored with mine, I ask Dad and he buys them for me straightaway."

She paused.

"And sometimes I say to myself that I hate Lucy. But to lose my sister, like you lost Frank . . ." She blinked. "That would be unthinkable."

"Do you still think making a memory box is a waste of time?" Ruth asked.

"No," Amy said firmly. "I actually think it's a brilliant idea!"

"It's good to keep things from your past so you can cherish your memories," I told her. "But it's also important so that future generations, just like you and Lucy, can learn and understand as well."

"Everything that means something special to me will be going in mine," Amy said, taking her pen from her mouth and getting up from the sofa.

"Well, just remember," I said, reaching up and taking her hand in mine. "Whatever you put in your box won't just be a reminder of your childhood, it'll be something for your grandchildren to enjoy, too."

"Just like I've enjoyed today, Grandma," Amy said, reaching down and kissing my cheek. "Do you have a shoebox somewhere, Mum?"

# Poppy's Day

### by Pat Posner.

W HO remembers what we talked about yesterday?" Miss
Howarth asked.

"Poppy Day, miss," one of William's classmates said.
William hadn't been at school yesterday because he'd had a
bad tummy ache. But he knew about Poppy Days. They
were the days his mum went to work and Gran met him out of school with
Poppy, Great-gran Amelia's Shetland sheepdog. They went to Gran's and he
talked to Grandad and Great-gran Amelia and played with Poppy. That's why
he called Monday, Wednesday and Friday a Poppy Day. No. He couldn't call
them that any more because Poppy, Poppy was . . .

William bit his lip hard and tried not to cry. He missed Poppy so much.
Missing her gave him a pain. A bit like the tummy ache he'd had yesterday –
except the missing Poppy pain was a bit higher up than his tummy and it
made it hard to breathe.

"And on Poppy Day," Miss Howarth said, "people wear a poppy badge to
show everyone they're thinking about and remembering loved ones who
died."

I didn't know there would be a special day for people to remember Poppy,
William thought. I remember her every day. I remember how she held up a
paw to say "hello" and how her tail wagged so hard it made it windy.

Miss Howarth was saying something about muddy fields now. William
closed his eyes and saw a picture of him and Poppy running around the field
near Gran's house. That was muddy sometimes and then Poppy got mud all
over her feet and legs, and Grandad had to wash it off. Poppy hadn't liked that
much.

"Now," Miss Howarth said, the sound of her voice making William jump
and the pictures behind his eyes disappear, "now we're going to make poppy
badges and you can wear them on Poppy Day to show everyone we're
thinking about loved ones who are no longer with us."

William decided he'd make a really good Poppy badge and wear it all the
time so that Gran and Grandad and Great-gran Amelia would know he was
thinking about Poppy. Maybe he could make badges for them, too!

"William. Are you listening?" Miss Howarth asked.

"Yes. We're going to make Poppy badges for Poppy Day," he said. "Please
can I make four, Miss Howarth? One for Gran and for Grandad and for Great-
gran Amelia as well, 'cause they've got lots to remember and think about.
I'm going to their house after school so I can give them their badges then."

138

Illustration by Mandy Dixon/Thinkstockphotos.

Miss Howarth nodded, smiling.
"I'm sure they'd like that, William."

*　*　*　*

"So, what did you do at school today, Billy-boy?" his grandad asked.
William sighed.

"I got a bit mixed up. Everyone was talking about Poppy Day – the special day for remembering the people who died in the wars. I thought they were talking about our Poppy and when Miss Howarth told us to make poppy badges, I drew pictures of her." William gulped. "It made me feel so sad, Grandad . . . " He rubbed his hand over the tears rolling down his cheeks.

"Oh, William." Grandad looked sad, too. "Did Miss Howarth explain what she'd meant by Poppy Day?"

"First she asked me if Poppy was a dog who'd died or done something

139

very brave in a war. And I told her Poppy died two weeks ago. So then she 'splained that Poppy Day is when we remember those who died fighting in wars."

"Seven is a bit young to understand," Great-gran Amelia said from her chair close to the fire. She was nearly one hundred years old and William loved her loads.

He looked across at her.

"All the others in my class understood because they'd talked about it yesterday when I wasn't there. I think I understand now, but how can I remember people who died in wars when I didn't know them? I can't think about them when I don't know what they looked like. I know what Poppy looked like. That's how I could draw such good pictures of her for the Poppy badges I made."

"What happened to the badges, William?" Great-gran Amelia asked.

"Miss said I could bring them home. They're in my backpack."

"Well, bring them here. I'd like to see them."

"I drew Poppy asleep for you," William told her. "'Cause she liked to sleep with her head on your feet."

"She knew my feet get very cold. It felt so good when she put her head on them and warmed them up."

Great-gran Amelia smiled as she gazed down at her badge.

"Hello, Poppy," she said. Then she looked at William.

"When I pin my poppy flower badge on, I'll wear this next to it."

"But she didn't fight in a war. Poppy Day is for remembering those who died in a war."

"Linda," Great-gran Amelia said, "go and fetch that big box of photos from my room, dear."

William watched his gran go. It always sounded strange to hear her called Linda.

"That's a great idea of your great-gran's, Billy-boy," Grandad said. "There'll be some photos of my dad in that box. I never knew him because he died in the World War Two just before I was born. He would have been your great-grandad."

"So I could think about him on Poppy Day 'cause when I've seen a photo of him, I'll know what he looked like? I'll have to tell Miss Howarth that at school tomorrow."

"I think you'll have more than that to tell her, William," his great-gran said with a wink. "Just you wait and see."

✳   ✳   ✳   ✳

"So." William stared at a browned photograph of a man in a soldier's uniform. "This is my great-grandad. And I never knew him because he died fighting in a war and this . . ." he carefully touched the dog sitting next to his

140

great-grandad in the photo ". . . this dog who looks just like Poppy and was called Poppy, too, was in the war with him?"

"For a little while, yes," his great-gran replied, "and then, when she came home to me, we used to knit the combings from her hair into balaclavas and mittens and send them to the troops fighting in the war to keep them warm. So this Poppy didn't die in the war but helped a lot in the war effort."

"She had puppies after the war, didn't she?" Grandad asked. "And we kept one. She was called Ruby."

"We always kept a girl puppy from every litter," Great-gran Amelia said. "It's a shame Poppy, the Poppy you loved so much, William, didn't have any puppies. But she was the ten-times-great-granddaughter of the Poppy in this photo. So we can all wear the badges you made for us on Poppy Day and remember the first Poppy, and the Poppy who was –"

"Her ten-times-great-granddaughter and who looked just like her!" William interrupted in his excitement. "So I was sort of right when I thought Poppy Day was an extra special day for remembering her!"

"You were," his gran said, ruffling his hair. "But there's another poppy badge you could wear, too. It's a purple poppy from Animal Aid. If I see a collecting tin, I'll put some money in and get us one each. A purple poppy is worn next to the red poppy to remind people how animals, not only dogs but cats, pigeons and horses and other animals, too, worked and helped in wars and are still doing so today."

THE next day at school, William told Miss Howarth and his classmates all about the first Poppy dog and how the Poppy he'd drawn pictures of was related to her. Then he told them about the purple poppy and what it was for.

"So now," Miss Howarth said, smiling, "let's all make purple poppy badges to wear beside our red ones."

William smiled, too. He'd pinned the badge he'd made for himself yesterday on to his sleeve and he looked at the picture of Poppy with muddy paws and legs. He remembered how Great-gran Amelia had spoken to the picture of Poppy on the badge he'd made her and thought he'd do that, too.

"I won't get mixed up today, Poppy," he whispered. And, although it still hurt, and still made him sad when he remembered he'd never be able to stroke her or play with her again, talking to her picture made him feel a little bit better.

As he started drawing a purple poppy, he felt glad he'd be able to wear three badges for Poppy Day. A red one to think about his great-grandad and others who'd died fighting in a war, this purple one to think about Great-grandad's Poppy dog, whose hair had gone into making warm clothes for soldiers, and – William looked at the badge on his sleeve again – and this one. The picture badge of the first Poppy's ten-times-great-granddaughter, who had been, he felt sure, the best dog in the world. ∎

## *Beddgelert, North Wales*

SOMETIMES called Snowdonia's loveliest village, Beddgelert's stone-built dwellings, inns and hotels are surrounded by the finest scenery in North Wales. The village, in keeping with its location in the Snowdonia National Park, is picturesque and unspoilt. Snowdon, the highest peak in England and Wales, dominates the skyline a few miles to the north. The mountain, at 1,085 m (3,560 ft), is the highest peak in Britain south of the Scottish Highlands. It forms the centrepiece of a dramatic upland range of rocky summits known as the "Horseshoe" – the plunging screes, razor-sharp ridges and mountain lakes make it a magnet to outdoor enthusiasts and lovers of spectacular scenery. The peak gives its name to the 845-square-mile Snowdonia National Park. Beddgelert is one of the favourite bases from which to climb Snowdon and many of its surrounding peaks. ■

*Illustration by Norman Lee.*

# Wee Sadie Perjink

## *by Amanda Young.*

NOW, let me see if you'll do."

Mary Davidson's daughter and husband stood to attention for inspection. They were due to visit Miss Mirren Murdoch, and everything had to be just right.

"Will you never learn, Willie?" Mary scolded gently as she refastened the buttons on his cardigan in the proper holes.

The father winked at his daughter, and when his wife reached up to wipe away a smudge of shaving soap he'd missed, he leaned down, gave her a smacking kiss then stood back to attention, looking all innocent.

Little Sadie started to giggle.

143

"Willie Davidson!" This time the scolding was severe. "We'll be late for our visit to Mirren. You know what that means!"

"Aye! Mair soor faces," Willie answered and Sadie laughed outright as he imitated Miss Murdoch's stony face becoming even grimmer.

"Don't encourage him, Sadie," the mother warned. "He's enough trouble as it is."

But she flashed her boisterous husband a grin before turning to inspect her daughter. Then she nodded in satisfaction at the neat blue serge coat, the white ankle socks and the matching red scarf and gloves.

"I suppose you'll do," she allowed.

It didn't do to give weans too much praise, but inside she glowed with pride. Her father called the child "Wee Sadie Perjink", and she thought how perfectly it fitted. Always neat as a pin and smart as paint, her lass was a daughter to be proud of.

Adjusting her hat and giving a final look at the banked-up range fire, Mary had turned to open the door when the bell gave an imperious ring.

"Oh, michty," she said, irritated. "Wha can this be?"

It was a telegraph boy. Mary looked alarmed; telegrams often meant bad news.

"Here. Let's have that." Willie Davidson took the orange envelope and tore it open.

"It's Hammy," he told her. "He's fallen off a roof! His sister wants us to meet her at the Royal Infirmary."

"Uncle Hammy?" Sadie cried in fright.

Her mother squeezed her shoulder, knowing that the lass had a great soft spot for Hamilton MacDougal, who had been in the "sodgers", as Sadie called it, with Willie.

"Is he going to be all right?" Mary asked of her husband now.

"Aye, in time," Willie told her. "He's broken his thigh bone. He'll be on his back for weeks and weeks. It's serious enough. Still, he might ha' been deid!"

"Since we're ready, we can go to the hospital right away," Mary said. "Oh, but what about Mirren Murdoch?" She frowned, wondering what to do. "Sadie, you'll have to go by yourself and explain what's happened."

Her daughter was open-mouthed, terrified at the responsibility suddenly thrust upon her.

"You can take the tram," Mary went on. "Willie, gie her a penny for the fare."

He dutifully reached in his pocket, found a couple of pennies, and slipped them to his daughter with another wink, while Mary pretended not to notice. She knew fine well that Sadie's eyes would be sparkling with mischief to match his, and fine she knew he'd given her twice as much! The penny left over from the tram would be enough to buy a pokey hat from Pacitti's café. But Mary smiled to herself and let them keep their little bit mischief.

144

"Just say a friend's been taken ill, Sadie. No need to go into details," she said, knowing that Sadie would understand.

A LONG time before, Mary had let her daughter into a sad matter. "This goes no further," she warned Sadie, "but you had better know about it so you don't say something out of place. You've heard tell of your da's aunt Ella?"

Sadie nodded.

"Well, she was housekeeper to a Mr Murdoch, a widower with one daughter. That daughter was Mirren Murdoch. In time Mr Murdoch married Ella, so that makes your da Mirren's stepcousin. When your da and Hammy came home from the war, the four of us – them, me and Mirren – cleeked up in a foursome, and what great times we had!" Her eyes shone at the recollection.

"But they were still bits o' laddies, and though our hearts were set on one another, we couldn't get married until we'd some money behind us." She paused and shook her head. "Then Ella and her husband passed away, and overnight Mirren became weel aff. She wanted to get married right away, but Hammy wouldn't have that. Said he'd earn for both of them. They rowed and parted, and though there's never been anyone else for Hammy, she has never spoken his name since."

"But if Da and you were such good friends with her, and he was kind of a cousin, how come you don't get on very well now?"

Mary was surprised to hear such insight from her wee daughter, and she chose her words carefully.

"It's no' that I fell oot wi' Mirren, but she inherited some real cousins along with the money. She hardly knew them before, but they've been all over her ever since. Aunt Murdoch this and Aunt Murdoch that. That lot have had plenty from Mirren, but I will not get the name of being a sponger. That's why we visit her only occasionally. You must always call her Miss Murdoch. I will not have you smarm over her."

* * * *

On the way to Miss Murdoch's, for the first time without her parents, Sadie thought on this story. It saddened her, but it also intrigued her, for Sadie was a film fanatic. She never missed a Saturday morning at the "wee" pictures, where a penny bought her a seat in the first six rows and she could thrill to the exploits of Tom Mix and Flash Gordon.

Sometimes, when her da was flush, he took Sadie and her ma to the "big" pictures on a Friday night. There Sadie was in her true element, watching films dripping with romance and glamour. She wept for forsaken wives, groaned for misunderstood fiancées, and ached for lost loves. And when in the final reel it all came right, she left with her soul uplifted and her face

▶ all smiles at the thought of true love being fulfilled.

If ever a story called for a happy ending, surely it was this one between her beloved uncle Hammy and Miss Mirren Murdoch! As she went for her tram, Wee Sadie Perjink wondered if she mightn't just nudge Fate in the proper direction . . .

Miss Murdoch's flat wasn't far from Sadie's as the crow flies, but the two homes were worlds apart. The big flat had five rooms, including a parlour with a three-piece suite upholstered in horsehair that prickled the back of Sadie's legs. There was also a bathroom holding a cast-iron bath with a gas geyser ready to spout steaming hot water!

Sadie's home had only two rooms – a living-room and a good room, used only on special occasions. The family washed at the jawbox in the scullery,

and shared a toilet with the other families on the landing. Her parents slept in the kitchen recess, while she had a bed in a press off the good room.

At the door, she carefully wiped her shoes and rang the bell. The door was opened by Miss Murdoch's skivvy, fourteen-year-old Christine, who until a year before had been fond of playing peevers with Sadie in the school playground.

Since this was an occasion, the girl was dressed in a black frock, a white maid's cap and a fancy wee pinnie to match.

"Oh, my!" the girl exclaimed. "Ye're awfu' early, Sadie. Ah hivny got the kettle oan yet."

"Don't you worry, Teenie; I've come to say we'll no' be needing tea today."

Miss Murdoch's imperious voice cut across the conversation.

"Who is it, Christine?"

"It's only me, Miss Murdoch!" Sadie called out as that austere lady came into the hallway.

"Oh! It's you, Sarah. Where are your mother and father?"

"Please, Miss Murdoch, they had to go to the hospital. A friend had an emergency." Sadie repeated her mother's words. "My ma and da had to go to see him. Ma said I should come at once and save you making the tea, and hoped you wouldn't be put out."

Mirren Murdoch looked down at this young visitor.

"I am indeed sorry to hear that, Sarah."

Although Sadie was only twelve, she could hear that this concern was genuine. Her own affectionate nature warmed to this austere lady. She couldn't be all bad, surely.

The forbidding woman seemed unsure of what to do with the small figure in front of her.

"Have you had lunch?"

Wee Sadie Perjink knew that lunch was something posh people had, instead of the dinner they had in her own home.

"Oh, yes," she said, nodding firmly. Then, thinking this needed explanation, she added, "Ma always makes sure we get soup with lots of bread and jam to follow before we come here."

Miss Murdoch's severe expression changed to one of surprise.

"Why does she insist on that?"

Sadie found herself unsure how to answer. Her ma had not prepared her for such a question. She started hesitantly, but her innate honesty could not be denied.

"It's just that we get such a nice tea here," she blurted out, "and Ma says we mustn't seem greedy. So we've to fill ourselves up before we come."

Mirren Murdoch's face was a study. For a long time she had wondered why the Davidson family seemed to eat so sparsely, while her own cousins almost ate the carpet.

Suddenly she had a mind to find out more about this quaint child who usually did not have a word to say for herself.

"Would you like to have tea with me?"

Astonished by this, and mindful of her ma's injunctions, Sadie spoke diffidently.

"I would like that fine. But would it be all right?"

"Of course it would. I will explain that you agreed to keep me company."

"Me? Keep you company? Oh, crivvens!"

There was a curious twitch of Miss Murdoch's lips that might have been the beginning of a smile.

"Give Christine your coat, then, and go into the parlour. I shall join

148

you in a moment."

Sadie knew from the films just how to act. She handed her outdoor things to the skivvy in the regal manner as became a gracious lady. Still, though, she couldn't for the life of her forbear to warn Christine.

"See and hang ma coat up by its catch, now, and no' by the collar, Teenie."

Mirren Murdoch made a curious snorting sound. Mistaking it for a suppressed sneeze, Sadie, still in movie mode, enquired grandly, "I do hope, Miss Murdoch, that you are not sickening from some serious malady?"

Sadie wasn't sure what a malady was, but she had heard a similar remark in a costume drama once and thought it very impressive. At that, Miss Murdoch buried her face in her handkerchief and hurried into her bedroom.

"Jings!" Teenie said in alarm. "Ah think she'd better tak' an Abdine powder afore it gets ony worse."

Sadie nodded in solemn agreement. The miraculous properties of those powders were known in every tenement in the city.

SADIE was ushered into the parlour. It was the first time she had been in that grand room on her own. Free of her mother's watchful supervision, though careful to touch nothing, Sadie wandered around, imagining what it must be like to spend life in such grand surroundings.

Miss Murdoch joined her before long, apparently restored to normality. Teenie followed behind, bearing the grand silver teapot used on such occasions.

Well schooled by her ma, Sadie sat down on the prickly sofa and waited for Miss Murdoch to do the honours. As she went to pour tea, the lady paused.

"Would you prefer a glass of milk, Sarah?"

But Sadie was thoroughly enjoying playing her part and would have none of such childish vituals.

"Oh, no, thank you!" she exclaimed in her best Hollywood voice. "Tea quite is my favourite beverage."

She had longed for an occasion to use that word.

Miss Murdoch's lips twitched again as she poured the tea.

Sadie was secretly pleased to find that this stern lady had added enough milk and sugar to make the kind of baby tea she really liked.

"That will do, Christine. I shall attend to my guest now."

Her guest, indeed! Sadie was flattered.

"Now, what would you like to eat?" Miss Murdoch indicated the splendid array of goodies laid out.

Sadie worked her way through plain bread and butter, fruit loaf and pancakes from an array of plates. Then she was faced with a three-tier cake-stand. Had her mother been present, Sadie's course would have been clear. Having filled up on plain stuff, she'd have been allowed one fancy thing. But her ma wasn't here, and this presented a problem.

"Sarah, is something wrong?" Miss Murdoch's voice was concerned.

"Oh, no. There's nothing wrong. It's all scrumpshous. It's just that you've been to a lot of trouble for us Davidsons, and I'm not sure whether I should eat more, to show how much we appreeshiate this, or if I should stick to Ma's rules about having one fancy thing only after the plain stuff."

Mirren Murdoch gazed at her young companion in astonishment. Such honesty was so different from her father's relatives.

"It is always a compliment to the hostess to eat well."

"And it would be all right with Ma?" Sadie had to be doubly sure.

"If your mother asks, I shall tell her that you behaved with complete propriety."

Wee Sadie Perjink hadn't the faintest notion what propriety was, but the word had that very grand ring to it that she so adored.

"Crivvens!" she breathed, and started on the first tier of cakes.

WEE Sadie Perjink finished the last bite of a cream meringue, took a final sip of milky tea, then sat back on the horsehair sofa in such a state of bliss that she no longer even noticed the prickly ends jagging into her legs.

"That was . . ." Sadie paused. She knew she must do justice to the hospitality she had just received, but none of the fanciful words she could dredge up from her memory quite fitted it.

"It was lovely." She sighed. "Just lovely."

The simple expression came from the heart, and Miss Murdoch had to reach for her handkerchief once more.

"There is something I must attend to," she said, sniffing. "Will you excuse me for a moment?" Miss Murdoch spoke to Sadie as one adult to another.

"Please, take your time," the girl replied with equal gravity. "I'd love to look at your books, if that would be all right?"

"Of course. You may borrow any volume you wish. Bring it back when you're done, and choose another."

"Can I?" Sadie was thrilled, and once again felt there was someone much nicer trying to get out from under this stern exterior. That must have been the someone Uncle Hammy had loved.

She opened the glass doors in the upper half of the bookcase, picked some books out, and sat cross-legged on the floor to see which she fancied. Putting one aside to take home, she turned her attention to the wooden doors below.

Sliding one open, she found shelves full of old fashion magazines. She lifted out one pile, and leafed through them, laughing at the styles of the twenties. Lifting out another lot, Sadie found, carefully hidden away at the bottom, a cardboard folder. Opening this, she was astounded to behold the portrait of a young soldier in the same uniform her da had worn – the kilt, the

150

bonnet, the sporran worn with swagger and pride.

Though the picture had been taken years before, she recognised him at once. It was her uncle Hammy. Tutored by all the romantic films she'd ever seen, she knew what this meant.

"She still loves him! But she canny bear to look at his photie, nor can she abide to tear it up!" Sadie's soft heart was filled with pity. No wonder poor Miss Mirren Murdoch had a soor face.

"It's enough to make a body greet!" she sobbed, doing that very thing herself.

At that moment Mirren Murdoch came back into the room and was astonished to find her little visitor kneeling amongst a scatter of magazines in floods of tears.

"Whatever is the matter, Sarah?"

"Oh, I canny bear it. Here you have been in love wi' my uncle Hammy a' these years, and now him in the hospital!" Sadie waved the portrait at her.

"How dare you?" Miss Mirren Murdoch was furious. Then the full meaning of Sadie's words struck home. "You mean it's Hamilton MacDougal that your parents have gone to see?"

Her face turned suddenly white. She groped for a chair, and had to sit down.

Wee Sadie Perjink knew these symptoms and they confirmed her suspicions. Her mind raced as she strove to turn the situation to advantage.

"He's to be kept in on his back for weeks an' weeks an' weeks, wi' never a sweetheart to visit him."

"I'm sure Mr MacDougal has lots of sweethearts."

"Never. He has only one true love. He's aye talking about Mirren. And he carries a picture of her in the back of his watch."

Uncle Hammy's pocket watch struck the hours, and he often let Sadie play the tinkly chimes. She knew fine that the picture in the case was that of his prize-winning homing-pigeon, "Mirren of Mugdock". The girl's strict code of honour would never have her lie, but this was a desperate situation. Besides, the look on Mirren Murdoch's face made this perjury worthwhile.

That stern lady's face had turned from white to red. She rose to her feet, unsteady.

"I've been such a fool," she whispered. Then, in a normal voice, she said, "I have enjoyed your visit, Sarah. Don't forget your book."

The visit was clearly at an end.

At the door Christine helped them both with their outdoor things, then came the time to say goodbye. Sadie knew she should hold out her hand and say something formal, but suddenly this wasn't good enough. Her ma would have a fit if she said Aunt Murdoch, but she longed to be on a different footing with this lady with the tear-bleared eyes.

She turned to her hostess.

"Would it be all right if I called you Auntie Mirren?"

Miss Mirren Murdoch was no fool. She knew very well what her cousins were up to when they called her Aunt Murdoch. But she was very lonely and put up with their faking because it gave her a feeling of at least some kind of family.

She noted again the utter sincerity of this quaint child. It was an offer of the kind of affection for which her heart craved.

Without hesitation, this usually unbending lady knelt down and opened her arms to let Sadie rush into them.

"I would love to be your auntie Mirren. And you will be Sadie from now on."

Wee Sadie Perjink wandered home, her mind so full of the afternoon's happenings that she clean forgot her pokey hat from Pacitti's café.

THAT night the Davidson family was having a quiet hour's reading before bed when the doorbell rang.

Who could it be at this time of night, Mary wondered as she went to answer the door. Her astonishment increased when she found Mirren Murdoch standing on her mat.

Mary Davidson was not often lost for words, but this time her voice failed her.

"Aren't you going to ask me in?" Mirren asked brusquely.

Mary's manners came back at once, along with a sudden presentiment. Her daughter's account of that afternoon's visit had been unusually brief.

"Is this about something Sadie has done?"

"It is."

With deep foreboding, Mary ushered her visitor into the gaslit room with its three chairs in front of the fire.

Willie and Sadie rose and offered the best chair in welcome.

"Now, Sadie," Miss Murdoch said. "You come and stand by me while I tell your ma and da just what you've been up to."

Mary looked at her husband helplessly. What had their daughter done?

"And how," Mirren Murdoch continued serenely, "I will need you to be a flower girl at my wedding, just as soon as I can get yon muckle idiot back on his feet. Climbing roofs at his age, indeed!"

After a stunned pause, the little kitchen exploded in shrieks of laughter and cries of delight mingled with tears as the three adults rekindled their old friendship. Then the kettle went on the hob, cups were looked out and the misunderstandings of years washed away, while Wee Sadie Perjink sat on her new auntie's knee with a dreamy smile on her face.

"That was better nor ony picture!" her mother heard Sadie whisper to herself later, after she had washed her face in the sink. "And, best of all, this is just the beginning." ■

# Mandy 1971

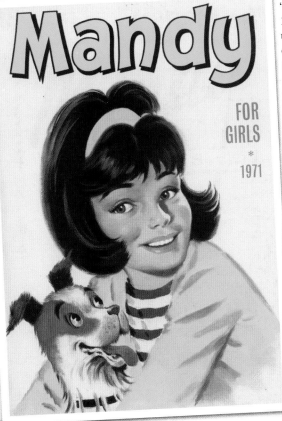

**THE** popular girls' comic "Mandy" first came out in 1967, though it wasn't until 1971 that readers could enjoy the first annual.

This was the year that the UK switched to decimal currency, family favourites "The Two Ronnies" and "The Generation Game" were seen on TV for the first time, and "Top Of The Pops" audiences tried to stop themselves warbling the lines from Clive Dunn's "Grandad", Middle Of The Road's "Chirpy-Chirpy-Cheep-Cheep" and "Benny Hill's "Ernie, The Fastest Milkman In The West".

The fashions on the pop shows began to be reflected in the illustrations in "Mandy" and other girls' comics. Teenage heroines sported jeans and the popular long, layered hairstyles of the time. Mandy herself retained her sweet Sixties-style bob and Alice band, while her trusty hound, Patch, remained his cute, slighty scruffy self throughout the pair's funny adventures.

Stories, stories and more stories were the order of the day in the "Mandy" annual. The heroines of the comic strip tales were an independent bunch. Shop assistant Sally in "Something Borrowed, Something Blue" was determined to become a fashion designer, thirteen-year-old Judy battled a cat burglar in "King Cat" and the phenomenal "Wonder Girl" had a surprise in store for an unscrupulous businessman. Longer reads and short, funny stories completed the picture, making "Mandy For Girls 1971" a certain treat for girls everywhere. ■

# Moving Home

### by Jenny Alexander.

HIS is not how I imagined it would be. So much for happy families!

Believe me, I didn't expect it to be easy, setting up a new home with a new husband and a teenage step-daughter. But this is only day one and already I've fallen at the first hurdle.

Today we moved into our brand-new home – me, Joe and his sixteen-year-old daughter, Georgina. It still smells of paint and is full of energy-saving devices – apparently it's very important to Georgie that we try to save the planet. It's cold and I fiddle with the controls on the state-of-the-art, eco-friendly boiler, but I can't make them out.

Joe will be back in a while. He's taking his brother, who's very kindly been helping us lug furniture into place all day, home. And if I don't sort myself out soon, he'll come home to a freezing cold house, full of unopened boxes and with no food on the table.

Food – and my mention of it – that's when it all started to go wrong. I sit at the kitchen table. The room is cold and bare, gloomy with no curtains yet at the windows. How on earth will I explain to Joe that I've already upset his daughter, causing her to storm off to goodness knows where? I try to console myself with the knowledge that Georgie knows this part of town like the back of her hand. She'll probably be in the warmth of some friend's house by now, eating something comforting, gobbling it down as if she's starving and hasn't eaten for weeks, and then she'll just breeze in through the front door as though nothing has happened.

Actually, perhaps that's a bit harsh – Georgie is great. She works hard at school, does her homework with no fuss and loves her dad to bits. She's an only child, an adored daughter, and I worried at the beginning how I would fit into their little world.

I met Joe at the Christmas food market in Bramfield. They hold it every weekend from November and I've been going for years. I run a little catering business from home, though nothing too ambitious. I've found a niche in the market for people who mostly want to do their own catering but just need a little bit of help for special birthdays or anniversary parties, christenings, and, of course, at this time of year, when families get together. All except for mine at this moment in time!

I love the Bramfield Christmas market. It's a great place to pick up festive treats – old favourites like decorated gingerbread men and new ones like Christmas pudding muffins. Joe saw me buy a dozen of them last year.

"I'm going to take that as a recommendation," he said. "They must be

154

*Illustration by Kirk Houston/Thinkstockphotos.*

good. I'll take two, please," he said to the stallholder.

"Only two?" I replied cheekily. "Two won't be enough."

"Ah, they're just for me and my daughter," Joe said, looking a little embarrassed as if he didn't really know why he said that.

I, in turn, didn't know what to say, so I just smiled, noticing his kind, caring face and warm smile with just a hint of sadness behind his eyes.

"Well, I'm sure you'll both enjoy them and you can always come back and get some more."

Joe smiled and we stood there for a while, not wanting to leave but unable to think of anything else to say. Joe broke the silence first, grinning at his cheesy remark.

"So, do you come here often?"

"Yes, actually, I do," I said eagerly.

"Would you, by chance, be here next Saturday? Perhaps at about eleven o'clock, at this stall, buying Christmas pudding muffins?" he asked.

"I most definitely will."

The following week I got there just a few minutes before Joe and bought two muffins and two teas which we enjoyed as we wandered around the market. We did the same thing every Saturday all the way up until Christmas.

That was almost exactly a year ago and things have moved on pretty swiftly from then.

I STARTED to cook for Joe in my little cottage. He learned of my passion for food and was more than happy for me to experiment on him. He told me that he'd raised Georgina alone since she was ten years old, after her mother died following a short illness.

I remember the first time I met Georgie. She and her dad were due at my place at six o'clock. I was nervous and had spent ages choosing the menu. With some help from Joe as to her likes and dislikes, I decided on chicken soup to start, pasta carbonara as the main and then white chocolate and raspberry cheesecake as dessert.

I needn't have worried – it was a great success. Georgie was thrilled that I'd

## Odds And Ends

I HAVE a useful little drawer
That's home to many things:
Buttons, twine and pens galore,
Old beads and curtain rings.

Tubes of glue, a rubber band,
Receipts and batteries,
Candles, matches, notebooks and
Assorted mystery keys.

Tools for spectacle repair,
Spare labels, ties and clips . . .
Bits that don't belong elsewhere –
At my fingertips!

I long to throw them all away,
But, oh, it's guaranteed
That soon I'd find, to my dismay,
They were just what I need!

– *Emma Canning.*

made such an effort in her honour. She kept saying how posh the table looked, laid properly for all the courses, with wine glasses and linen napkins that she said were much too nice to wipe your mouth on.

She was studying Food and Nutrition among her GCSEs and showed an enthusiastic interest in what I'd cooked. At the time I thought it was great that we had a shared interest; I imagined us cooking together, growing close.

At this point in time, I'm not sure that we can get back on track ever to becoming close.

Joe and I married two weeks ago. We decided against a honeymoon, choosing instead to go on a family holiday later in the year. I moved into Joe's place for the few days before we were all to move into our new home together.

Georgie was very quiet this morning. That in itself should have alerted me that something was wrong. She was dragging her feet and just being generally unhelpful, and by the time we got to the new house, my patience was wearing thin. I made a last ditch attempt to gee her up.

"Georgie, love, why don't you take some of your things up to your room? We'll try to clear some of these boxes, shall we, before your dad gets back? Tell you what, we'll work at it for twenty minutes and then stop for tea and chocolate cake, what do you say?"

And that's when she exploded.

"Tea and cake? Is that all you think about? You think that's the answer to everything, but it isn't!"

"Georgie, love, whatever's wrong?"

But it was too late; she'd already grabbed her coat and was out the door.

Now, admittedly, I am of the philosophy that a nice hot cup of tea and a piece of cake will help to comfort most people. But in my heart of hearts, I don't really think Georgie is angry with me for this.

Something is seriously wrong. I can see that now. I've been stupidly blind to anything other than organising the packing up of two houses and making sure everything is sorted. I haven't given a thought to a bewildered sixteen-year-old who was leaving the only home she had ever known, full of memories of her mum.

I dig into a nearby box and take out a few random items: a kitchen clock, a stack of tea towels and a *Home Sweet Home* plaque I bought in a garden centre for our new home. I smile sadly and place it back in the box. It's no good, I can't concentrate and decide to go for a walk to clear my head.

I WALK to the end of the lane, leaving my new home behind me. The Christmas market is off to my left and, as it has always been a happy place for me, I head in that direction. I stop at a small park where a group of teenagers are piled up on a bench, all vying for a little space so as not to be left out. I casually glance over but can see instantly that Georgie isn't there.

What would I do if I saw her right now? More importantly, what would be the right thing to do? Even though I've never been a parent, I know I want to give her the biggest hug and reassure her that everything will be OK.

I arrive at the market and it's getting dark. The lights are on, long lines of multi-coloured light bulbs up high and twinkly fairy lights highlighting each festively decorated stall. The food-sellers will be doing a great trade with their mince-pies, roasted chestnuts, jacket potatoes and hot spicy cider. This will be a lovely place to come as a family one day, I hope.

I wander around the market for a while, looking at the delicious treats on offer. I half-heartedly buy a few items and then wearily decide to head back home. I dread facing Joe. What a terrible start to our life together.

I walk to the edge of the market and smile wryly as I find myself right next to my favourite stall – the one that sells the Christmas pudding muffins. I decide to buy some, still a little hopeful that the day will end on a happy note. My heart sinks into the depths of my boots as I see the empty tray. It feels like a bad sign. The stallholder recognises me with a warm smile and sees the direction of my disappointed gaze.

"Sorry, love, I sold the last few a while ago. Do you want some mince-pies instead?"

"No, thanks." I shake my head.

I walk home and I can see our house in the distance now. As I unlock the door and step inside, the first thing I notice is the glorious warmth that envelops me. I'm puzzled because Joe can't be home yet, but as I walk through to the kitchen, I see Georgie fiddling with the boiler controls.

"Ah, you fixed it. That's great," I say, relief flooding through me to have her back home.

She turns to face me, smiling tentatively, looking relieved.

"Yeah, it's nice and warm now."

I walk towards her and see that she's unpacked some boxes and laid the table ready for supper. She's done a grand job; everything is neat and perfectly placed.

"This is lovely," I say. "Thank you."

"And best of all," she says, grabbing a bag off the kitchen worktop and taking out a cake box. She opens the lid to reveal three Christmas pudding muffins. "I got the last three," she says, looking utterly pleased with herself.

I can't stop myself from laughing, but then stop abruptly as she abandons the cake box on the table and runs into my arms, giving me a tight hug. I'm speechless and overwhelmed with emotion.

"I'm sorry about earlier. I didn't mean it. I was just a bit sad about leaving."

"You've nothing to be sorry for." I stroke her hair and hold her close. "It's OK to be sad."

Georgie looks up into my face.

"I'm glad we're all here," she whispers.

"Me, too, and I hope this will be a happy home for all of us."

She smiles and at the same time the front door bursts open and Joe rushes in.

"Wow, it's cold out there!" he calls out. "Nice and warm in here, though," he adds, coming into the kitchen.

Joe smiles happily as he washes his hands in the sink.

"I see we're all set for supper. The table looks great."

Georgie beams as I tell her dad that it was all her own work.

"Well done, love. I see we have our very favourite Christmas pud muffins. Shall I put the kettle on and make us all a nice cup of tea?"

Georgie and I exchange a smile.

"That sounds like a lovely idea. Georgie, do you want to help me clear some of these boxes out of the way?"

She dives into a nearby box, almost disappearing inside it.

"Yeah, we've got so much stuff to put away." She lifts out the *Home Sweet Home* plaque. "Where shall we put this?"

"You decide." I'm intrigued as to what her answer will be.

"It should go right next to the front door. I reckon that, with all your home-baking and cake-making, this will always be our home, sweet home." ▦

# Desperate Times

*by Val Bonsall.*

"L OOK," Jordie says, nodding at us grimly, "these are Desperate Times, lads. They could come under cover of night and who'd see 'em? We need someone here all the time. And I've done my fair stint."

Kev and I look at each other. We've been good mates since we were boys. I was best man at his wedding last month. He's more reason than me to get back home. And my work – a little gardening business – is more flexible than his.

"I'll stay on," I say.

"Good on yer, Matthew." Jordie gives me what I imagine he thinks is a hearty pat on my back and nearly breaks it. Doesn't know his own strength, that one.

I reach for my mug of tea, then promptly put it back down again. Tin mugs might look practical, but the handles of ours get too hot to lift the wretched things up!

Nonetheless, I'm soon reaching for it again, desirous of its heat. Darkness is falling and the temperature, never high, with it. Snow isn't forecast, but it's cold enough.

I sigh. Like Jordie said, desperate times.

The Back of Beyond, my mum calls this area, but it's Paradise to those of us in the climbing club. My gran understands. It's from her that I got my love of nature and the remote spaces still to be found round many towns.

It's true, though, there's a lack of amenities! Which is why the club's so lucky to have the little hut where we're presently huddled.

The problem is, how long will we continue to have it? The hut is on land belonging to the Hall, a huge old house. Though we're outside their fenced-off area, some previous owner, some time in the past, bought the bit of ground where we're sited – that much is clear from the old documents.

Recently the Hall was used by an educational organisation, and they never bothered us. But they left and some kind of financial consultancy firm took over the lease. And they've turned out to be Trouble.

They sounded OK at the start. They planned to run courses for their staff there, outward-bound-type things where firms transplant their office staff out into the wilds and get them doing outdoor oursuits for a few days. Improves

160

*Illustration by L. Antico.*

team spirit, apparently.

They started by bussing the staff up in coaches, but our club has learned that their intention is for people to start using their own cars. And for that, they need to construct a car park . . . right where our hut is.

Our initial reaction was, they can't do that! But the wording in the agreement is complicated. There's a phrase which gives permission to be *ongoing for as long as it survives*. We say the "it" is the club. The company says it means the hut, hence our fear that they might resort to knocking the hut down, blaming it on a storm or something, when none of us is there. They could then say it's ceased to "survive", so the permission would have expired. And they can get on with building their car park.

161

As a precaution, while the legal position is sorted out, we're trying to ensure someone is in the hut all the time. Jordie, as he's said, has been here since last week. Kev and I came up yesterday. Kev will go home tonight, and Jordie in the morning. After that, for a few days, it'll just be me. Luckily I'm fine with my own company.

NEXT morning, after a shared tin of sausages and beans heated on our trusty old Primus, I accompany Jordie to the main road, from where he can get a bus into the village, then another to the station.

On the way we spot a group from the Hall, clambering up the hillside. We can tell right away they're from the Hall and not the usual hikers.

"It's the designer anoraks that give them away," I comment to Jordie.

"And the daft hats," he replies, pointing over to a little stand of trees. Sitting with her back against the rough trunk of one of them, looking rather pitiful, is a young woman in a striped woolly hat with flower shapes sewn on to it.

Jordie's right, it is a daft hat. But she looks cute. Pixie-ish.

"You OK?" I ask.

"I tripped," she says, "and did my ankle in."

She's half-removed her clearly brand-new boot, and I can see her foot is already starting to swell.

"Needs bandaged up," a voice from behind me says. I turn to see Philippa from the village post office, out with her dog. "Do you have first-aid stuff in your hut?"

"Of course –" I break off as Jordie beckons.

"I'm not sure you should let her in the hut," he mutters when I reach him.

"Why not?"

"She might be a spy from the Hall, keeping tabs on us!"

"So you're saying we let her hobble all the way to the village with Philippa?"

He looks back towards her.

"No. But . . . be careful, Matthew."

With that, he nearly fractures my shoulder again with one of his friendly pats and strides off.

"Can you walk?" Philippa asks the pixie. "Do you need to lean on us?"

She elects to lean, and we do a sort of five-legged manoeuvre back to the hut with her hopping along between us in a somehow dainty manner, though how you manage that in great clumpy boots is beyond me.

"What's your name?" I ask, expecting Tinkerbell or something similar.

"Eleanor."

\* \* \* \*

Having checked I've got everything required, Philippa leaves me to dab Eleanor's ankle with witch hazel and wrap it in a stretchy bandage.

162

"That'll give it some support," I say. "But I'm surprised one of your team isn't given a first-aid kit when you start out."

"They were. It was my line manager. I shouted on him, but he just ignored me – they all did – and carried on."

"I thought the purpose was that you helped each other, and bonded and stuff? Improved your team spirit?"

Suddenly any resemblance to a gentle pixie disappears as Eleanor's eyes flash angrily.

"Team spirit? Hah! Everyone's just out for themselves in that place. It's the corporate culture – you're encouraged to be like that. To outdo whoever's at the next desk. You've to be a certain type to survive there." She sighs. "A friend warned me, but I needed the job."

She looks tearful as she picks up the mug of tea I've made for her. Then she lets out a cry – I forgot to tell her to watch the handle.

"Oh, I hate it here!" she says with feeling. "I wonder if they'll send us home early if it snows?"

I laugh.

"Like at school?"

"I'm leaving anyway if it does," she continues grumpily. "When I was a kid, I was in a car accident in the snow. Ever since, I've just to see a flake and I go all funny."

She's quiet for a moment.

"I did once walk through a whole field of it. But that was when I was out looking for my little brother. We were coming back from my aunt's and it snowed, and we stopped the car because I felt sick, and he wandered off. I guess if someone's important to you, you'll do anything for them."

She pulls the sleeve of her jumper down to protect her fingers and takes a sip of her tea.

"What about getting back to the Hall with your ankle?" I ask. "Can you phone someone?"

"No. When they send us out on these treks, we mustn't take our mobiles or any money. We're supposed to think on our feet if anything goes wrong, and improvise. My mobile can't get a signal out here anyway! Give me the city – the crowds, shops, bright lights, streets where the snow never settles . . ."

"My mobile works OK here," I reply, feeling the need to defend my area.

"Could you order me a taxi to the Hall, then?" She fishes deep into the sock on her unhurt foot and produces a £20 note.

"I thought you said . . .?"

"I smuggled one out for emergencies."

I wonder briefly if that's a bit, well, spy-like. Was Jordie right?

"I'll take you on my motorbike," I tell her.

We finish our tea in silence apart from the odd yelp due to the mug handles, then she turns to me.

"Could I borrow your phone to make a call? Obviously I'll pay for it."

I hand it to her and go outside to give her some privacy, but I can't help overhearing some of what she says. It seems she's awaiting a decision on something, which won't be available now until tomorrow.

She pokes her head round the door.

"Matthew, would you mind if they used this number to call me here tomorrow?"

I say OK, but once she's hung up I ask how she'll manage to get away from whatever they've got planned for her group tomorrow.

"It won't be difficult. I bet nobody will even have missed me today!"

She's right. When I drop Eleanor at the Hall, her colleagues are also returning. No-one seems to have missed her. And though she's limping, no-one bothers to ask why. They're not a team – I see that right away. Like she said, all out for themselves.

SHE arrives mid-morning. That day's exercise, she explains, consists of them being taken out in Land-Rovers in smaller sub-groups and dumped, miles from the Hall, to find their own way back.

"I told them I couldn't possibly walk that kind of distance, not with my ankle. Health and safety, I said. They couldn't argue with that."

"Your ankle's still sore?"

"No, I was playing on it, to be honest. I am normally honest but . . ." She breaks off, looking for the right words.

"Desperate times?" I say, thinking of Jordie's assessment of our situation.

"Exactly." She frowns. "I thought about you last night."

I thought of her, too, actually. How her arms had felt round me on the motorbike.

"Do you live here?" she continues.

"No." Sure I can trust her, I tell her our fears for the hut, and how we're presently trying to ensure it's always occupied.

She nods.

"I wouldn't put it past them."

"What time do you expect your phone call?" I ask after we've chatted a while.

"Not until the afternoon. I'm sorry, am I keeping you from doing something?"

"Only from going out for an hour. Nothing too energetic. You can come with me, if you like."

I'm not sure how keen she is on this idea, but she comes along. Her eyes widen with wonder as we watch a peregrine falcon plummeting that way they do from the sky. In the conifer plantation she's fascinated when I tell her I've seen red squirrels there. While we're out, she collects a few bits of fallen branches. Back at the hut she's found a box of battery-operated fairy-lights that someone must have brought up some time.

When we get back, she adorns the branches with the lights and switches

164

## Truly Blissful

THE night is truly blissful
When drips the moonlight pale,
Weaving among the shadows
To form a dappled trail;
When pipistrelle are flitting
Among the woodland trees,
And tawny wings are gliding
Across the quiet leas;
When birds, in peaceful slumber,
Breathing the cooling air,
Are rocked by gentle breezes
That softly whisper there.
A night that's so enchanting,
I'll linger just to hear
The soothing little echoes
Which haunt the atmosphere.

– *Alice Jean Don.*

them on. It makes the place look cosy.

Her phone call comes through. I watch her face in the soft glow as she says again and again, "Wonderful!"

"I've got a new job," she tells me when she's finished, "with a nice company – a charity!"

Then she throws her arms round me and gives me a hug. Just from excitement, I know.

"I'll tell that lot at the Hall as soon as I get back," she says gleefully, "and I'll be on my way home tonight! I've got holidays to cover my notice."

Next morning, when someone bangs at the hut door, I think it must be my replacement, here earlier than I expected.

But it's Eleanor.

"I thought you would be away by now," I greet her.

"No, I decided to stick it out. We're going tomorrow anyway, so it's only today I've to get through. Trouble is, I can't keep making my ankle an excuse, so if you see some idiots swinging on ropes tied to trees, one of them is likely to be me!"

Later I wander down to where they are, and Eleanor and I manage to sneak off for another walk. As we say goodbye, I ponder asking to see her when we both get back home. We don't live far apart at all, as it turns out.

But then I think, what's the point? All my spare time, I'm out somewhere like this.

And she has said it herself: she's a city girl who loves the shops and bright lights.

THAT night it finally snows. When I open the door in the morning, the sparkling beauty of the transformed world takes my breath away.

Gazing about me, I see a coach pulling up by the Hall, come to collect Eleanor's group. The main roads must be OK, then.

My breath catches again, but for a different reason. Someone is struggling through the snow towards the hut . . .

"I . . . came . . . to tell you . . ." Eleanor says, speaking breathlessly at first, "that apparently there was a meeting about your hut yesterday. You're right – the hut can stay as long as you have a club. There's absolutely nothing they can do."

This time, I'm the one who throws my arms round her. Just in delight, you understand.

"There's more," she says when we're inside. "They've decided the Hall isn't for them. So they're clearing off."

I grab the chance to give her another hug. It's then that I remember how she feels about snow. And yet she came all this way in it . . .

I remember something else she said.

*I did, once, walk through a whole field of snow . . . looking for my little brother. I guess if someone's important to you, you'll do anything for them.*

"I'm glad you're here," I tell her, "because I was wishing I'd arranged to keep in touch."

"Why didn't you?"

"I wasn't sure you'd want to. The way I am – into the countryside and all that, whereas you . . ."

"Those walks we had?" she interrupts me. "I really enjoyed them. I think it depends who you're with. I'd be happy to do it again – with you."

I pass her a mug of the tea I've made us, nearly burning off my finger-ends in the process because I'm so distracted.

"Well, I can see the benefits of cities, too," I say. "They've got cafés where you get your drinks in proper china cups! So I'd say there's room to compromise."

"Plenty," she agrees with a grin, squeezing up along the bench where she's sitting. "Plenty of room." ■

166

*Illustration by Mandy Murray/Thinkstockphotos.*

# The Tinsel Fairy

## by Anna Buxton.

'D always been a hoarder. Every surface in my house was covered in something, be it family photographs, sprigs of dried flowers from special bouquets arranged in souvenir vases from long-ago holidays, or cute knick-knacks and whatnots given by friends.

Objects had always held memories for me. I still had the cotton-reel animals and lopsided pencil holders made by the children when they were at school – not on display these days, but safely tucked away in shoeboxes in the wardrobe in what used to be Katrina's room when she was little.

167

▶ Certificates for Brownies, badges for swimming and books presented as prizes for achievements of yesteryear were stored up in the attic in a tea chest, next to one which was full of baubles for the Christmas tree we brought down each December. These days it was on the pretext of it being for the grandchildren's amusement, but my husband knew that the tradition of decorating the trusty, everlasting spruce was all about recalling my own children's childhood for me.

As I squirted polish on the patch of sideboard pushed clear of trinkets I paused momentarily, duster in hand, and glanced across to the carrycot where Katrina's youngest lay peacefully sleeping, her tiny thumb thrust into her rosebud mouth. Then I turned back to the sideboard, rubbed, and – hey presto – an ice rink! This seemed rather appropriate as the first ornament to go back on the clean area was a miniature skating couple, bought by Simone the year we took her to her first ice pantomime. She'd been captivated by the hypnotic tale of "Sleeping Beauty" and her brave handsome prince.

Bending at the knees, I lowered my face to the level of the skaters. Half-shutting my eyes, I imagined them gliding across the shiny expanse – she pointing a weightless leg out behind her, he with supporting hands firmly around her waist. I hummed a little tune, and to add a bit of movement to the scene, I slid the duster gracefully up and down the polished surface.

LOST in my daydreams, the sudden wail from the carrycot sent me jerking forward, and the duster shot out of my hand. Hastening to my feet, I went across to the baby.

Katrina, no doubt, would have snatched her up immediately, and fed her, or changed her, or paced up and down. But I, with the wisdom gained from experience, merely rocked on the carrycot handle, and, lo and behold, my granddaughter's eyelids grew heavy again, and I tiptoed back to my cleaning.

Now, where was that duster? Gingerly, I reached down the back of the sideboard. It was very dark down there, and there was no knowing what else might be lurking. I took a deep breath, gritted my teeth and grabbed. Up came the duster, but I'd pulled something else up as well! Cautiously, I took a peep.

I blinked in disbelief. I could hardly believe my eyes. It was the tinsel fairy! I'd lost all hope of ever seeing her again.

Tenderly, I smoothed out her bent little wings and straightened her twisted wand. This was the beloved tinsel fairy that had graced our festive tree every Christmas apart from this one, when she'd been pronounced officially lost.

All of a sudden, I found myself back at the grammar school Christmas party from which I'd got her, when I'd been on the brink of turning sixteen. Standing in a corner of the assembly hall was an enormous pine tree which the Upper Sixth had swathed in tinsel for the series of celebrations they hosted, form by form, for the rest of the school. Someone had fashioned the fairy that was to become mine, and had perched it up on the top.

In the adjoining dining-room, through the gaps in the partition, I could make out paper chains hung from the ceiling, and tables laden with sandwiches, crisps and jellies. There was an announcement that there would be a disco, with records played by the school's very own groovy resident DJ.

"Oh, blimey! I can't dance!" I remember exclaiming bleakly to my best friend, Sharon, as the hall's lights dimmed, leaving just a glow on the stage.

"'Course you can, Lynne!" Sharon yelled encouragingly as the pulsating beat of the first number took over. "All you have to do is wiggle around to the music."

To illustrate her point she elegantly raised her arms up in the air and started fluidly swaying her hips, like one of Pan's People performing on "Top Of The Pops".

In her trendy black and white shift, she looked fabulous. She was even wearing false lashes, and had accented her eyes with dark liner. How I'd wished I had parents like Sharon's. My stuck-in-the-past mum would have had a fit if I'd worn an outfit as short as the one Sharon had on.

Not that I had money for the latest fashions, anyway. I sighed as I watched Sharon jigging about uninhibitedly. My dad worked on a farm, and money was scarce. When coats were stripped off in the cloakroom, and Mary Quant followers and Twiggy look-alikes abounded, I sported a jumble-sale dress from a decade before.

Still, I was determined to have a good evening as I crept into the hall.

AT that time, I hadn't known that uncoordinated me would be faced with the mortification of being expected to dance.

Making an effort to please Sharon, I waggled my arms a bit and shuffled my weight self-consciously from one foot to the other, praying that no-one was looking my way, until she was whisked away into the throng by the most desirable heart-throb of our year. I switched my attention to eyeing up my heart's desire. For up on the stage was the focal point of my passions, the school's resident DJ – the luscious head boy, Kevin.

From the concealing dark of the hall I stared up to the stage where my gorgeous long-limbed, dark-haired idol was spotlighted, putting on records and oozing appeal. I could hardly believe my good fortune.

Among those of us who didn't have boyfriends, Kevin had quite a following, though no-one, I reckoned, had the hots for him as keenly as I did. My heartbeat quickened whenever I passed him in the corridor; I tingled all over at the sound of his voice. When I hung around beneath the common room window at break times, I positively swooned every time he came into view. And now I was blessed with the chance to ogle him to my heart's content.

"Are you OK?" Sharon suddenly materialised beside me.

"I'm fine." I nodded dreamily.

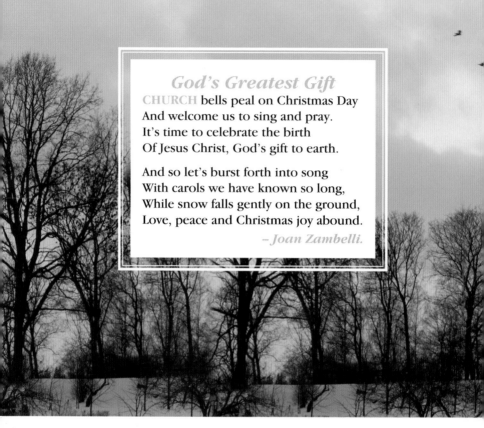

### God's Greatest Gift

CHURCH bells peal on Christmas Day
And welcome us to sing and pray.
It's time to celebrate the birth
Of Jesus Christ, God's gift to earth.

And so let's burst forth into song
With carols we have known so long,
While snow falls gently on the ground,
Love, peace and Christmas joy abound.

*– Joan Zambelli.*

"I don't want you to think I've deserted you in favour of Nick!" she yelled through the music.

From my blissful trance I beamed a contented smile and vehemently shook my head.

I did the same when Theo, a new boy in our class, who had recently come back to England after a long spell of living abroad, asked me to dance.

"Can't dance!" I mouthed back at him with what I hoped looked like well-mannered regret. Theo was an OK kind of boy and I didn't want to offend him.

He'd sorted out my bicycle chain when it had slipped off its sprocket the previous week just as I was pedalling out of the school gates. He'd got his hands all oily, and I'd dreaded to think what his mum was going to say about the black greasy patches all over his hanky. But Theo hadn't seemed bothered. Either that, or he'd played it down to save my embarrassment at causing him trouble.

He was much the same over my insistence that I couldn't partner him

because of my two left feet.

"No, really, I couldn't. Thanks all the same," I firmly refused when he held out an inviting, supportive hand and started jigging around encouragingly.

I felt a pang of guilt as I watched him go back to his mates, but he hadn't made a big thing of my turning him down. He'd just cocked his head to one side and shrugged.

EVENTUALLY the music was turned off and Kevin announced the start of the party games. The first was to be "Crossing The River", which was a contest in which the boys carried the girls around the perimeter of the room, then over two chalked lines that represented the banks of a river. My eyes were out on stalks as he continued explaining that the winners would be the last remaining pair not caught in the river on the occasions when the horn sounded.

Had I heard correctly? Were the boys actually going to carry the girls? In their arms?

Pupils started to pair off – some keenly, some more reluctantly. And at last I saw my chance. Suffering as I was from a permanent longing to feel Kevin's arms around me, I wasn't going to let this opportunity pass me by. Bold as brass I dashed up to the front of the hall, grabbed him by the arms, and beseeched him to partner me.

I can still remember the humiliation of being taken aside by Priscilla, the head girl, and being told that the Sixth Formers did not take part in the games and that I was embarrassing Kevin. She even accused me of standing and gawping at him all evening instead of taking part in the disco. Time stood still. My face was burning hot. I found out what people meant when they said that they wished the earth would open and swallow them up . . .

A N insistent crying from the carrycot brought me back to the present with a jolt. It must be feeding time for the baby by now. I stretched up and secured the tinsel fairy to the top of the bauble-covered, everlasting spruce tree where it belonged.

Reaching into the carrycot, I picked up my adorable granddaughter and put her over my shoulder, rubbing her back soothingly. As I carried her into the kitchen to warm up her bottle, I reminisced about how tactfully Theo had asked me to partner him in the game that evening all those years ago. He'd casually posed the suggestion as if he hadn't just witnessed me, moments earlier, making a complete fool of myself. We'd had a laugh and a giggle as he'd careered across the chalk lines with me in his arms.

That evening had ended a thousand times better than it had begun.

"You'll never guess what I found!" I challenged my husband, who was sitting at the kitchen table. His head, now grey-haired but still lovely, was bowed over the local weekly newspaper he was reading intently.

"Tell me," he invited, laying the paper aside.

"The tinsel fairy, would you believe!" I responded, all smiles, passing our granddaughter into his arms so I could heat up her bottle.

Reaching out for the kettle, I sighed.

"I'd have hated to have lost her for good. She brings back such special memories of that school party, where we had our first kiss."

"I think I sensed your love of souvenir knick-knacks even at that early stage." My husband chuckled, his eyes twinkling kindly. "There's no doubt my giving her to you set our relationship off on the right footing," he teased.

"You'd have looked a right fool carrying a fairy made of tinsel home yourself," I retorted as if I'd been offended, but unable to stop myself smiling.

"I consider she was mine by rights!" my darling Theo protested. "After all, I was the one who lugged you across that river so we could win her."

"I'm so glad you did," I murmured as he drew me close and made the stars shine for me with his loving, meaningful kiss. ■

172

## Commando 1989

**DESPITE** the comic first appearing in July 1961, it wasn't until 1989 that the first of only two Commando annuals was published. Military themes were evident in the entertainment industry at the time – Kenneth Branagh's film of Shakespeare's "Henry V" was one of the most popular releases that year.

Meanwhile, television audiences more used to shedding tears of laughter were moved to tears of a different kind when the poignant ending to the final series of "Blackadder Goes Forth", set in the Great War, was broadcast nine days before Armistice Day showing the well-loved characters charging into battle for the last time. Perhaps the thoughts of war weren't so surprising for a year in which Margaret Thatcher, George Bush Sr and Mikhail Gorbachev had declared an end to the Cold War, 40 years after the freezing of relations between the superpowers.

Continuing the theme, in seven colourful comic-strip stories the "Commando" annual followed the adventures of men caught up in WWII. From the headstrong young Newcastle lad forced to grow up fast after working the seas in an east coast collier, to the seasoned heroes of the skies over enemy territory, the stories convey the rush of adrenalin and ties of comradeship felt by the men on active service in those long-ago days.

The links to a shared history, and to the family members who lived through the campaigns, are all there to be seen and felt leafing through the pages of that first "Commando" annual. Little wonder, then, that the stories remain so popular today. ■

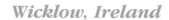

# Wicklow, Ireland

WICKLOW is a county diverse in landscapes with a varied coastline of long sandy beaches, hidden coves and rugged cliffs. In County Wicklow you will find a unique blend of classic country houses in large, well-tended estates characterised by lovely gardens and rambling parkland and wild countryside. Known as the Garden of Ireland, County Wicklow is one of Ireland's true scenic treasures with its magnificent mountains, tumbling waterfalls and dramatic lakes.

County Wicklow has long been a favourite with filmmakers. Referred to as "The Hollywood Of Europe", Wicklow has attracted filmmakers since the time of the black and whites. "Braveheart", "Excalibur" and "Michael Collins" were all filmed here, but the village of Avoca in Wicklow is perhaps best known as the filmset for the BBC TV drama series "Ballykissangel". ■